THE PROTECTORS

UPS & DOWNS

AVALANCHE
on the prairie

by **Grant McKenzie**

**Diverse
City
Press** Inc.

Diverse City Press (La Presse Divers Cité)
33 des Floralies
Eastman, Quebec   J0E 1P0

450.297.3080   www.diverse-city.com

Illustrations by Averie Moppett

McKenzie, Grant

Avalanche on the Prairie

1) Teasing
2) Down Syndrome
3) Children's Literature

ISBN 1-896230-20-2

Dedication

To Kailey – Who will always know
dreams can come true.

To Karen – Who already knew.

Table of Contents

Owl was never given the chance to fit in.

From the moment the doctor lifted him by the ankles when he was mere seconds old, the world had gaped open-mouthed at the folds of thin, wing-like skin that connected his arms, from armpit to elbow, to the sides of his torso. No adult spoke the word that, in later years, the children whispered just loud enough for him to hear, but he knew they were all thinking it.

Freak.

As if having unflappable wings wasn't bad enough, Owl had also been born with a severe cleft lip that made his mouth and nose resemble the curving hook of a bird's beak. And his hair . . . "What was God thinking when He designed your hair?" his mom often asked. Owl's hair was long and curly, its mixture of orange, brown and pale yellow resembling the plumage of the creature his mother named him after.

It also didn't help that Owl needed glasses and the only ones that seemed to fit his pie-shaped face were thick and circular, making his eyes seem huge and perfectly round.

Owl *was* a freak and there was nothing he could do to disguise it. His clothes were bulky because he needed the room under his arms to store the delicate folds of wing-like skin, but they were also over-washed and worn because his mom couldn't afford anything new. All he knew of his father was a brittle, yellowed postcard sent from a faraway port. Wherever he was now, he didn't even know a son had been born.

By the age of 10, Owl had been on the receiving end of

enough cruel remarks to scar even the most hardened adult. He had never been able to make friends, yet Owl didn't feel angry or resentful. He found solace in the fact he had a mom who loved him very much, and he also had the most precious gifts of all: curiosity and imagination. Now those were things that could never be taken away from him, no matter how hard some people tried.

(2)

"Hey, Freak. Are you too wimpy to use the shower?" teased a danger-filled voice.

Owl looked up from the long row of wooden benches that sat in front of an equally straight row of gunmetal grey lockers and met the boy's challenging stare. It was like looking into the eyes of a skeleton that had shrink-wrapped his skull in sandpaper-rough, pimple-pocked skin. His cheekbones stuck out below dark hollows that contained even-darker eyes, and his nose was like the thin-edge of an axe. The only features that told you he was actually flesh and blood were the heavy, shoe-polish black eyebrows and a thick wave of hair that stood out from the top of his skull like a rooster's crown.

The boy's name was Rodney Elvis Brown, one of the cruel kids who seemed to derive great pleasure from making Owl's life a constant struggle. In his first few days of school, and with the aid of a sharp punch to his left eye that bent the frame of his glasses, Owl had learned that you never call Rodney by his first name. He only answered to Elvis.

Rodney had a towel wrapped around his waist and his coal black hair was wet from the shower. Gym class had barely ended and Rodney's group of cling-on pals had staked their claim in the doorway of the shower stall - all the better to tease and torment every shy and insecure kid in the class. Owl, as usual, was their favorite target.

"I'm just waiting," Owl answered, lowering his gaze.

"I'm just waiting, what?" Rodney demanded. His wide mouth, that seemed crammed with too many teeth, curled in a sneer like he had just stepped in something foul.

Owl looked up, confused. "I don't understand."

"I'm just waiting, SIR!" Rodney yelled, spittle flying from the corners of his mouth.

Owl looked down at his hands again, a sly grin crossing his face that he knew he should ignore. But how do you fight such an easy setup?

"There's no need to call *me* Sir . . . Rodney," Owl mocked, his feet instantly hitting the ground as he ran for the door.

Heavy footsteps and screams followed in hot pursuit as Owl yanked open the door and fled down the hallway. He could hear Rodney's bare feet closing in just a breath behind when they suddenly stopped and a volcano of girlish laughter erupted around them.

Owl glanced over his shoulder to see Rodney clutching desperately at his drooping towel as he embarrassingly realized he was standing in a hallway filled with giggling girls on their way to next class.

Rodney glared at him, hatred pulsing in his eyes.

"You're dead, Owl," he threatened. "At three O'clock, your life is over."

Owl shrugged as though having his life threatened by a half-naked boy in the middle of a crowded hallway was the most natural thing in the world, and then he darted around the corner to safety. As soon as he was out of Rodney's sight, however, Owl felt his courage sink. What on Earth was he going to do when three O'clock arrived?

(3)

Sitting in the computer lab, still dressed in his gym shorts and T-shirt, Owl kept his eyes focused on the computer screen in front of him. The digital clock in the upper corner of the screen told him he only had 10 minutes of life left before the school day ended and Rodney's punishment began.

Suddenly, a tiny icon in the bottom corner of his screen began to blink. Owl clicked on it with his mouse and watched as the electronic chat program launched and a message popped onto his screen.

It read:

> *Locker room funny.*
> *Glad you got away.*
> *I wouldn't dare say anything.*
> *You give courage.*
> *-A Friend*

Owl was stunned. He had never had a friend before. And now, finally, because of a stupid moment of impulse, someone was calling him friend. Of course, it wouldn't do him much good. He only had - he glanced at the clock again - nine minutes of life left.

He typed a reply:

> *Thanks.*
> *Who are you?*

And back came the message:

> *Measles*

Again Owl typed:

> *What kind of name is that?*

The answer:

> *Me, same you. Elvis mean to me.*

Call me name. I pretend like it.
He leave me alone now.
I'm behind you. By teacher's desk.

Owl craned his neck around and saw a short, redheaded boy with pale white skin that was practically smothered in caramel-colored freckles. The boy waggled four short, sausage-shaped fingers in a wave as Owl studied his bright, oval eyes, small ears and nose, and a tiny, O-shaped mouth that curled up at the edges in a mischievous smile.

It was obvious he had Down Syndrome and Owl was struck by the similarity between his own physical differences and those of the boy. It was like looking in a funhouse mirror where all of Owl's harsh, jutting features (nose, mouth and chin) were softened and flattened.

Owl liked the look of him.

The boy winked and Owl grinned. Here was someone else, he thought, who knew exactly how it felt not to fit in.

Owl returned to his keyboard and typed:

Great to meet you, Measles.
I'm Owl and I only have seven minutes left to live.
- Owl

Back came the reply:

Elvis kill you?
What you to do?
- Measles

I don't know.
Any ideas?
- Owl

Run away again?
- Measles

5

I can't run that fast, but if I could get to my bike,
I can out-pedal anyone.
- Owl

There was a long pause before Measles replied.

Idea.

As the words formed on the screen, Owl thought, "Great, I'm about to take advice from a kid with Down Syndrome. I'm truly, truly desperate." Then he went back to reading Measles' idea.

Wait at back door.
Elvis coward, need friends there.
He'll be front door.
I'll get bike to back door.
Knock two times. You pedal like crazy.
OK?
- Measles

That sounds better than anything
I could think of.
Do you know which bike is mine?
- Owl

Seen you.
Red and brown.
- Measles

Yeah. It's supposed to be all red,
but rust seems to be winning the turf war.
Thanks for helping me.
- Owl

OK.

Friends?

- Measles

Owl couldn't believe his luck. He hadn't felt so happy in a long time. And even if the great escape fell apart and he was brutally tortured and murdered by Rodney, at least he would die knowing he had a friend.

Owl glanced at the clock again, and as if in response to the dread building in his stomach, the school bell rang.

All the students around him began to leap to their feet, stuffing homework and computer printouts into colorful backpacks, pausing only to shut down their computers. Owl rose to his feet slowly, zipped up his garage sale Batman pack from two movies ago and slipped it onto his back.

This was it, the last moments of his life. The other boys stared at him and whispered among themselves. A few of the girls giggled. They all knew he was dead meat.

"Don't fear," said Measles as he stopped beside Owl. His speech sounded thicker and slower than his typing had. The computer seemed to free him.

"Will you be able to do it?" Owl asked, sounding worried now.

Measles grinned. "I talk slow," he said in a deliberate, slightly garbled tone. "But I not dummy."

"I didn't mean that," Owl blurted instinctively.

Measles nodded. "You did," he said. "That OK. Trust hard."

Owl nodded, suddenly feeling embarrassed that he had judged Measles on his speech just as thousands of others had judged him on his looks.

7

"I don't really know much about Down Syndrome," he said apologetically.

"I don't know you," Measles replied. "But we learn?"

"If I survive the next few minutes that is," Owl added.

Measles grinned his mischievous smile again. "See you back door."

Owl lifted his hand to flash the OK sign, but Measles had already vanished into the noisy, departing crowd.

All alone, Owl tried to steady his nerves by breathing deeply. It didn't work.

"Snap out of it," he told himself. "You can do this. No one pedals faster than you — I don't think."

Truth be told, Owl was extremely fast on his bike. But at the same time, because he had trouble making friends, he had never actually raced against anyone before. So for that matter, he didn't really know if he was faster than any other 10-year-old boy.

"Is there something wrong, Mr. Hunter?" the teacher grumbled from behind his desk at the rear of the classroom. From the tone of his voice, Owl could tell the teacher didn't want to hear that his student was about to be murdered in front of a school full of bloodthirsty, Elvis-fearing kids.

Owl shook his head, gulped hard and made his way out of the classroom. The hallway was empty of students. News of the big fight had swept through the school like a tornado and they were all outside waiting for the freak's blood to be spilled.

Owl was sure half of them probably believed his blood would be blue or green instead of red just like theirs.

Without wasting any more time, Owl darted up the hallway to the back doors and waited.

That's always the toughest part: waiting. Thoughts go through your head without being processed by the part of your brain that's responsible for common sense. Owl's thoughts were no different and as he waited for Measles to knock on the door, he was suddenly filled with a thought too horrible to ponder. What if Measles wasn't his friend at all? What if he was one of Rodney's cling-ons and Rodney himself was waiting outside the back door? Measles might have set him up.

Owl couldn't bare the thought and shook it out of his head. Then came the double knock on the door.

Sucking in the last reserves of his courage, Owl swung open the door and almost passed out with relief when he saw Measles standing there with a grin that seemed to split his face from ear to ear. Owl's half-red, half-rust mountain bike was clutched in his hands.

"Come on, Owl," Measles whispered urgently. "You gotta go."

Owl nodded and jumped on the bike.

"What about you?" he asked.

Measles grabbed the back door before it could swing closed.

"I tell I saw you go," he said.

Owl nodded again. It was a good plan. Owl would have a head start and no one would know that Measles aided his escape.

"Thanks again, Measles," Owl said.

Measles grinned. "Pedal hard, Owl. Pedal hard."

Measles gave Owl's bike a push and watched it begin to pick up speed before he walked through the doors and slowly, very slowly, made his way to the front entrance to break the bad news to Rodney Elvis Brown.

CHAPTER 2
JUNKYARD

Owl was almost home when he saw them. Eight boys were lining the gravel driveway to the mobile home where Owl lived with his mom. Each boy sat astride a new 18-speed mountain bike, complete with dual air shocks and matching black and gold paint that glistened in the afternoon sun. They were bikes, Owl could only dream of.

"How could they have beaten me?" Owl asked himself. He had cycled hard across the fields, staying off the main roads so as not to be spotted, and used every shortcut he knew.

In response to his question, a black pickup truck with red and yellow flames painted on the front fenders crested over the hill and came to a stop in front of Owl's driveway. From the back of the truck, two more kids with gleaming black bikes climbed out and joined the gang of eight. As the truck drove away and the dust in its wake began to clear, Owl saw that one of the new boys was Rodney.

"Cheaters," Owl muttered under his breath.

Balancing his bike on the peak of a small hill, just a short distance from the driveway, Owl studied the gang with mounting despair.

If he couldn't go home, where could he go?

One option was to charge into the group, hoping the element of surprise would give him enough of an advantage to make it to his front door before they caught him. His mom wouldn't be home yet, but she never locked the doors so he wouldn't need to dig around for his key. Once inside, he could lock the door and wait for her to return.

10

His only other option was to hide out until it was dark enough to sneak home - hopefully by then the gang would have become bored and returned to their own homes.

His mind was made up for him when a yell erupted from the gang of ten. "There he is!" screamed one of the cling-ons, his accusing finger pointing directly at Owl.

Before Owl even had a chance to swallow, the ten boys were changing gears and pedalling their bikes straight at him.

Panicking, Owl yelped, turned around and started to pedal as fast as he could. The hills were steep and the unbroken paths were filled with ruts and boulders, broken branches and the odd rusted piece of lethal-looking farm machinery. The yells and war cries of the pursuing gang filled the air like ghosts from a long-ago Indian battle.

Owl kept pedalling, his trusty bike sending him soaring over gopher mounds and tearing through the sun bleached stalks of harvested wheat and once bright yellow canola. The wind tearing at his hair and clothes, the undergrowth snapping and cracking under his bald tires, the whelps of confusion and frustration swirling up from behind, all added to a rush of white-knuckled panic.

As he crested another hill, Owl lowered his head and pedaled even faster, his legs pumping like well-oiled pistons. His T-shirt billowed as he soared down the other side of the rise, the wind lifting him slightly out of the saddle and filling his eyes with sight-blurring tears.

Who said he couldn't fly? For just a moment, Owl felt himself leave his bike and soar into the clouds. He could almost imagine his flimsy wings expanding beneath his clothes, straining to lift him even higher.

Owl blinked his eyes as a feeling of weightlessness

suddenly washed over him and he noticed that he really had left the ground. He had been so wrapped up in the moment he hadn't realized he was soaring down the steep, rocky path that led to the lip of the town dump. And now, with his pursuers close behind, Owl found himself unable to regain control of his bike as the cliff edge rushed forward.

Before he had time to scream, Owl was lifted off his bike and sent tumbling over the edge and down to the junk-filled earth far below.

He landed with a crack that washed over him in a red wave and brought in its wake a heavy, mind-numbing darkness.

(2)

When he awoke, Owl could hear Rodney's voice.

"I can see his bike down there, or what's left of it," Rodney was saying, "but I don't see any sign of the freak."

"Maybe he's dead," added another voice.

"Maybe," Rodney agreed, "but if he was dead, we should be able to see a body."

Owl looked around at where he had landed and noticed he was covered in rotting and soggy cardboard boxes. The voices must be coming from the top of the cliff high above him.

"Should we climb down and look for a body," piped in another eager cling-on.

"Nah, it smells like elephant farts down there," said Rodney to the delight of his pals who laughed and slapped him on the back.

"We'll let him rot," continued Rodney, "and if he isn't dead, he'll wish he was the next time I see him."

Everyone laughed again. Then, by the snapping of twigs

and crunching of tires, Owl could tell they were pedalling away.

Slowly, Owl moved his arms and legs, testing for any broken bones or twisted ankles and wrists. Except for a sore head, he seemed to have survived in one piece.

He sat up and rubbed the sore spot on the back of his head. His bike was lying nearby, the front wheel twisted into a shape that was closer to a triangle than a circle.

He sighed.

"At least I survived," he said aloud.

"You may have survived, but look at my campsite," grumbled a tiny voice.

Startled, Owl swivelled his head from side to side, but he couldn't see anyone.

"Hello," he called. "Is anyone there?"

"No, you've gone completely crazy and my voice is just in your head," growled the voice indignantly. "OF COURSE THERE'S SOMEONE HERE!"

Owl jumped at the force of the yell and quickly scanned everywhere around him. He still couldn't see anyone.

"Where are you?" he asked.

"Good question," said the voice. "I was camping in that nice dry house you've just squashed into the size of a pizza box, but now where am I?"

Owl looked down at the cardboard box he was sitting on.

"This was your home?" he asked, not trusting his own words.

"No, it was my easy-bake oven. OF COURSE IT WAS MY HOME!"

Owl felt himself growing angry. "OK, that's it," he said. "I didn't know this was your home. And even if I did, it's

not my fault I fell on it."

"Whose fault is it then? You're the one who crushed it."

Owl turned to his left and peered into the side of the cliff face. There was a series of rabbit-sized burrows and the voice seemed to be coming from inside. This was getting weird.

"Look, I didn't jump," Owl explained. "I was being chased and I fell."

"Hmmmm," said the voice. "Who was chasing you, those boys on bikes?"

"Yes."

"Why?"

Owl sighed. "I don't know why. Their leader doesn't like me. In fact, he wants to kill me. The other boys just hang around him like a bad smell."

"They scare you?" asked the voice.

"Of course they do."

"Good, I never trust anyone who can't admit to being scared."

Owl shook his head and felt a tiny laugh build up from his belly. This was ridiculous. He looked down at the pile of crushed cardboard and sighed. "My name is Owl," he said. "If you show yourself, maybe I can help you rebuild."

"We don't show ourselves to humans," said the voice.

"Well this is your lucky day," proclaimed Owl. "According to those boys up there, I've never been human. To them, I'm just a freak."

"Why?" asked the voice.

"Look at me. Do I look human?"

"Well," said the voice, "you're shorter than some of them, your hair is a bit longer, nicer color though, and your face isn't all mushed up like theirs usually is."

15

"Mushed up," chuckled Owl.

"Yeah, your face has some character to it," said the voice. "I like it."

"You're the only one," Owl sighed.

"Are you kidding," declared the voice. "There's a whole slew of toylings down here that would love your face."

"Toylings?" asked Owl.

"That's what we call ourselves, but don't tell the humans. They'd boil us up and turn us into road tar or something worse."

Owl grimaced. "What could be worse than being turned into road tar?"

"I don't know," pondered the voice. "But if there is something worse, you can bet your copyright stamp that humans would think of it."

Owl nodded in agreement while his eyes stared into the dark burrows until he was sure he could see a tiny pair of eyes deep inside looking back.

"Are you going to show yourself now?" he asked.

"Only if you promise not to bite off my head or gouge out my eyes or rip off my arm or chew my feet or anything like that. Agreed?"

Owl nodded. "Agreed."

"Cross your talker box and hope to melt?"

"Sure, whatever you say," answered Owl, his face scrunched up in puzzlement.

"OK, don't be shocked," warned the voice as the tiny pair of eyes deep in the burrow grew larger until a foot-tall man in green khaki pants and light-brown shirt squeezed out.

"You're a doll," Owl gasped.

"Hey, don't be insulting," said the tiny man. "I'm a

toyling, but before that I preferred being called an action figure. For now, you can call me Joe. I'm the toylings' scout."

Owl looked him up and down. The toyling's close-cropped blond hair and beard was speckled with dirt and flakes of burnt plastic. His left arm was missing, the empty sleeve folded neatly and pinned to his shirtfront, and his brown plastic boots looked as though they had been melted onto his feet. His face had classic features though: a strong Roman nose, bright blue eyes, bushy eyebrows that were slightly darker than his hair and beard, and a strong mouth that looked as though it could use more laughter. It was a serious face, one you didn't want to mess with, but also one that seemed to instill trust.

Owl blinked his eyes a dozen times and rubbed the sore spot on the back of his head. "I must have hit harder than I thought," he said. "I have gone completely crazy. Toys don't talk and walk and live in cardboard boxes."

"Normally, no," agreed the toyling. "But the toylings are special."

"How so?" asked Owl, his attention riveted.

The toyling sat down on a rusted tin can and held up his feet. "You see these boots?" he asked.

Owl nodded.

"Do you know how they melted?"

Owl shook his head.

"Well," began the toyling. "My human owner tied me to a rocket, stuck it in the ground and lit a small fire underneath. Then he watched as the fire began to melt my boots and singe my clothes before igniting the rocket's fuse."

Owl grimaced.

"What chance did I have?" continued the toyling. "Well, before I knew it, the rocket soared into the sky. That was when I noticed this wasn't one of those reusable ones with the built-in parachute. Before I even had a chance to say a prayer, the rocket exploded. I got lucky and landed in a tree, but the cost was my arm and some severe melt spots."

"But you were a toy," Owl said, not believing his ears. "How did you come alive?"

"That's the easy part," the toyling continued. "Ordinary toys, those that are cared for and played with, always stay toys. But when we're tortured or dumped and discarded, some of us become toylings. I don't know how it works, I just know it does."

The toyling spread his arms to indicate the whole town dump. "This," he said, "becomes our home."

Owl stared at the tiny man, confused thoughts whirring around in his sore head.

"So there are more of you?" he asked.

"Sure," answered the scout. "We've got a whole community. Teddy bears, action figures, dolls, you name it. Last year's forgotten discards are the community's new members."

Owl rubbed his head again. "Am I dead?" he asked.

The toyling laughed. "Nah, you're just the first human we've chosen to speak to."

"*We've chosen?*" Owl asked.

The toyling nodded. "You were my mission," he said. "The junkyard needs the help of a human, although I didn't expect to have one fall on top of my head. That was unexpected."

"I don't understand. What do you mean *I* was your

mission?" asked Owl skeptically.

"Exactly that," the toyling said, jumping off the tin can and getting to his feet. "The toylings are in danger. I was asked to find a human who would be willing to help. You're it."

"But, but," Owl stammered. "What if I can't help? Or what if I don't want to?"

The toyling stared straight into his eyes. "Then I'll have to kill you."

"What!" Owl gasped.

The toyling started to laugh. "Just kidding. I've always wanted to use that line."

"Don't scare me like that," Owl protested.

The toyling laughed again. "OK, but before you decide you'd rather run away and hide from your biker friends than help a whole community of people in trouble, why don't you come see our village?"

Owl shrugged and nodded in agreement. "I suppose it's the least I can do since you're letting me hide out here."

"Good man," grinned the bearded toyling. "I knew I could count on you. Follow me."

CHAPTER 3
TOYLINGS

It took nearly ten minutes before Owl and the toyling reached a small hill in the middle of the dump. Along the way, they passed mountains of unidentifiable junk, rotting and rusting and baking in the evening sun.

Owl had never realized just how much stuff the townsfolk threw away. He saw old bicycles - one of which had a wheel that looked to be a suitable replacement for his twisted one - and tires, washing machines and grocery carts, clothes and mattresses, jars and bottles. He even saw the twisted wrecks of cars and an old John Deere tractor, flakes of green paint still clinging to its rusted frame.

"What a waste," Owl commented as they stopped at the small hill.

The toyling nodded in agreement. "Whatever the humans don't want or can't be bothered recycling, ends up here."

Owl looked around at the landscape, its mix of junk, garbage and dirt looking like a patchwork quilt designed by the color blind.

"Are we near your village?" Owl asked.

In response, the toyling knocked three times on a large wooden crate set into the side of the hill.

Much to Owl's amazement, eight tiny green hands pushed up one of the planks and four frog-like heads poked out, brightly colored masks covering their eyes.

"Hey, Joe. Did you bring food?" asked one of the frogmen. His accent sounded Russian.

"Is that all you ever think about, Mik?" Joe laughed. "No food, just a human."

The frogman's eyes bulged as he quickly looked up from Joe's face to see Owl. He gulped.

"Are you crazy, Joe?" the frogman asked. "Don't you know what they do to toys like us?"

Joe nodded. "I know, Mik, but Owl here is one of the good guys. He's come to help us out."

The frogman stared up at Owl and thought for a moment. "He's got a good face," he said finally. "It's not all mushed up like the rest of 'em."

"That's what I told him," Joe agreed.

The frogman seemed to come to a decision. "OK, Joe. Let me clear it with Teddy and get a few more hands to lift the door. We'll be back in five."

The plank of wood slid back into the crate as the four frogmen disappeared inside.

Owl stared after them for a moment before turning to the toyling. "Your village is inside the hill?" he asked.

Joe nodded. "Yeah, it's pretty cozy. We've dug tunnels throughout the dump so that we can stay underground most of the time. A few of us, like myself, come to the surface to look for lost travelers and any items we might need for expansion."

"Lost travelers?" Owl asked.

"Sure," Joe answered. "When a toy comes to life, he or she or it is usually pretty traumatized. Instinctively, they know to head for the dump, but we keep the village well hidden. As a scout, it's one of my jobs to find them and bring them back here."

Owl nodded. "How many toys, I mean toylings, live here?"

Joe stroked his beard in contemplation. "I don't rightly know," he answered. "Hundreds, thousands, maybe. I've

been here nearly twenty years and I've rescued an awful lot of toys in that time."

The wooden crate set into the hill began to shake and then slowly lift as fifty pairs of mismatched and multicolored hands pushed on it. Once the crate was standing on its side, Owl could see a large tunnel entrance beneath it.

"Let's go," said Joe. "Teddy will be waiting."

"What about my bike?" Owl asked, trying to buy some time. The tunnel looked dark and spooky.

"Mik and the lads will fix it with that new wheel we spotted," reassured the solider. "Come on, we don't have much time."

Owl gulped and followed.

(2)

Owl had to drop to his hands and knees to be able to crawl through the narrow tunnel. He didn't feel frightened until the door crashed down behind him and the tunnel was plunged into darkness.

"Joe!" he cried out in alarm. "Where are you?"

"Right here, buddy," the toyling said, his tiny hand gripping Owl's finger.

"I can't see anything," Owl said.

"It's okay, just let your eyes adjust. I've got some lights on the way."

As Owl's eyes slowly adjusted to the darkness, he saw a row of tiny sparking lights coming to life along the tunnel wall. He crawled closer and saw the light was coming from the clear plastic chests of a group of toy robots.

The name of the toy escaped him, but he was sure he had seen a commercial for it during Saturday morning cartoons: Rocky the Robot with light-up eyes and real sparking inner workings, or something like that. It wasn't a toy Owl had been interested in.

There must have been twenty robots lining the tunnel and they all looked practically brand new.

"Where did they all come from?" Owl asked as he crawled along behind the toyling.

"A full box of them was dumped a few months back," answered Joe. "They didn't even make it into a toy store."

"But why would somebody dump them?" Owl asked. "I mean, they're not the coolest toy going, but they could have been donated to a toy library or a children's hospital or something."

"Don't ask me," Joe said with a shrug. "You're the human. They could have been stolen, part of an insurance scam, or even just dumped by mistake. Heck, they even came with batteries included."

"Are they toylings now?" Owl asked.

Joe shook his head. "They never had a chance to be played with and experience life outside their limited-edition cardboard prisons. Without that experience, they can't make the change. They're just toys."

At the end of the row of sparking robots, Joe pulled aside a large canvas flap and Owl saw a gigantic cavern filled with glowing candles and oil lamps. The dirt walls were riddled with hundreds of small caves connected by a highway of rope ladders. Cloth curtains hung over windows of all shapes and sizes; doors were carved from strips of dried bark, each one interwoven with strands of painted straw and chunks of polished glass to create a unique design; everywhere you looked there were colorful, hand-dyed banners that hung down to expertly disguise the dreariness of the hard-packed mud. A lot of the homes even had elaborate wooden balconies with long poles sticking out above them and wet laundry hung on fishing line to dry.

In the soft glow that bathed the busy square below, Owl could see hundreds of toys chattering in huddled groups or busying themselves buying and selling pieces of tin and plastic or spools of wire and thread. The smell of fresh-baked bread and iced cakes filled the air with a tantalizing aroma.

Some of the toys were performing tricks while others clapped or sang encouragement. Others - looking suspiciously like rubber WWF wrestlers from an older era - were fighting each other in a makeshift ring while a throng of onlookers stood around and cheered.

Everywhere he looked, Owl saw mismatched, brightly clothed figures busying themselves in the same way humans did. The only difference was their size and the fact they all looked so different. Eleven-inch-tall fashion dolls were talking to five-inch action figures, alien-looking creatures were jamming with mop-haired humanoids, and there were even robots playing cards with scary-looking, B-movie monsters. Yet despite their obvious differences, everyone seemed to be getting along without trouble.

"It's like a giant medieval market," Owl gasped.

Joe nodded. "That's how we make a living. Bartering what we can find to those who need it in exchange for items they've found or made. Just like humans, we enjoy our creature comforts. It makes sense to trade the skills we have for those we don't."

Owl turned to him. "What do you trade for?"

Joe smiled. "I collect art," he said. "Couldn't paint a picture to save my life, but I've traded for a few nice pieces."

"Really?" Owl said. "You don't strike me as the artsy type."

Joe grinned. "I'm not always on duty, buddy. Sometimes I like to kick back and enjoy the finer things in life. Of course, if someone found a toyling-sized dirtbike, I just might discover a new passion."

The four frogmen came up behind Owl and the soldier. "Teddy is waiting," the one in the red mask said.

"Let's go, Owl," Joe commanded. "The chief requests the pleasure of your company."

(3)

Teddy sat in an old wooden rocking chair inside a green canvas tent. Scrawled in fresh white paint on the door flap were the words: War Council.

Owl's first impression of the toyling's commander was of a giant furry belly - the kind designed to comfort and lull children to sleep at night. But above the belly, the cuddly face had seen better years. Resting on a triangular nose stitched with multi-colored thread was a pair of brass spectacles, the left lens replaced with a worn leather patch. Both ears looked as though they had been chewed by a dog and were now folded and stitched with the same multi-colored thread.

Despite his roughed-up appearance, Owl could easily imagine how this bear was once a child's favorite stuffed toy.

Teddy stared at him through his one good eye, his mouth set in a determined line.

"Welcome to our land, human," said the bear, his authoritative voice booming like a thunderclap.

"Th-th-thankyou," stuttered Owl nervously. "My name

26

is Owl."

"Owl," said the bear, looking around at the twenty action figures standing or sitting inside the tent. Then he broke into a wide grin. "What a wonderful name, boy. It gives me hope."

"Hope, sir?" Owl asked.

"Call me Teddy," boomed the bear, his good eye twinkling. "We don't divide ourselves into leaders and followers here. Every toy is his or her own person. We depend on everyone's strengths. I may look like a leader inside this tent, but that is only because my skill is in the art of survival. What has our scout told you?"

Owl looked down at Joe. "Just that you need my help," Owl replied.

"Correct," Teddy sighed. "The humans are trying to poison our land and in so doing are threatening themselves to boot." Teddy paused and tried to smile as he lowered his voice. "I've been around enough of your kind to know you're not all bad. I don't believe, at least I don't want to believe, that what the humans are doing now has been authorized by your laws or your council."

"What are the humans doing?" Owl asked, his eyes wide.

Teddy sighed again. "We need to show you," he said and turned to the scout. "Joe, take him to the site and make sure he understands."

Joe nodded. "Consider it done, sir."

"They'll be back at sunset," Teddy continued, trying not to show his annoyance at being called sir. No matter how many times he had told the scout not to give him a rank, the toyling couldn't break his army mold. "So be careful."

Joe laughed. "I've never been caught yet, sir. I'm a vet,

remember?"

Teddy grinned back. "You may be a pro, Joe, but your cargo is only human."

"I can take care of myself," Owl protested.

"We'll see," said Teddy. "We'll see."

(4)

Joe led Owl through the tunnel and back outside. Owl's bike lay beside the wooden crate, his bent front wheel expertly replaced by the toyling crew. The sun was sinking fast and the rumbling in Owl's belly told him it was well past suppertime.

"I'll need to get home soon," he told the toyling.

"The site isn't far," Joe replied.

Together they scrambled over mounds of metal, dirt and garbage until they came to another large hill.

"Follow me," Joe said, scrambling up the slope.

Owl followed quickly behind and was surprised to see the peak looked down on an even deeper valley than the one they were already in.

"What's down there?" Owl asked.

"This is where they store the hazardous waste," Joe replied. "You'd be surprised at what they dump."

"Is it legal?" Owl asked.

"Yep," Joe replied with a shake of his head. "They can dump municipal waste, medical waste, hazardous waste, low level radioactive waste, incinerator ash, you name it. It's all supposed to be sealed so it doesn't leak into the ground water or poison the air, but there has been a lot of dumping lately that doesn't seem proper."

"What can we do?" Owl asked.

"For now, we wait," Joe replied, motioning for Owl to lie down hidden behind a metal carcass of an old fridge.

Shortly after the sun disappeared behind the hills, Owl heard a heavy rumble approaching from the north.

"What's that?" he asked.

"Just wait and see," Joe replied. "And keep out of sight."

As the rumbling grew louder, Owl began to notice odd twinkles of red and yellow approaching from the other side of the valley. Soon the twinkles grew into the lights of a half-dozen large trucks. The trucks stopped directly below Owl and Joe's lookout post. Two men jumped out of each vehicle.

Owl watched as the men ran to the back of the trucks, threw open heavy metal doors and began to unload three-foot-tall barrels marked with warning signs. Many of the metal barrels looked corroded and were oozing a disgusting green-brown slime. The men wore heavy rubber gloves and bright yellow masks that covered their faces from nose to mouth.

"What kind of masks are those?" Owl whispered.

"Air filters," Joe whispered back. "They don't like the smell anymore than we do."

Owl was about to ask, "What smell?" when it hit him. The stench burned his nostrils and churned his stomach.

"Yeee-uck!" he gasped. "What is that?"

"We don't know," said Joe. "But if it smells that bad up here, you just know it can't be sealed properly down there."

Owl covered his nose with his shirtsleeve and watched as the men hurriedly hid the barrels inside a large cavern dug out of the valley wall. Just as they were dumping the last barrels, Owl saw another truck approaching from the road.

This vehicle was much smaller than the others and Owl

recognized it as a black pickup truck. He gasped when he saw familiar red and yellow flames painted on its front fenders.

"Do you know that truck?" Joe asked.

"I saw it this afternoon," Owl replied with a nod. "It dropped off that gang of kids who were chasing me."

A man who looked like an older, meaner version of Rodney jumped out of the pickup and approached the other drivers. Owl couldn't hear what they were saying, but he just knew in his gut that they were up to no good.

"Have you seen enough?" Joe asked.

Owl nodded.

"Are you going to help us?" Joe continued.

Owl nodded again. "I'm not sure what I can do, but I'll try."

Joe grinned. "I knew we could count on you, Owl. Now let's get you and your bike home while the War Council decides our next move."

The next day at school, Owl had to be extra alert to avoid bumping into Rodney. He had almost made it through the whole day when, quite by accident, he made an error.

Stopping at one of the water fountains to catch a quick drink, Owl felt the notebooks under his arm begin to slide out of his grasp. Quickly, he fumbled to catch them, but he was too late. The books clattered onto the floor, spilling paper everywhere.

Trying not to panic as the hallway began to empty of students, Owl bent down to pick up the notebooks. As he did, a shadow fell over him. Owl gulped and looked up at the boy looming above.

"Need help?" Measles asked, bending down to collect a handful of the errant paper.

Owl heaved a sigh of relief. "Thanks, Measles," he said, "I was worried you were somebody else."

Just then, four more shadows fell over the squatting duo.

"Who were you expecting?" asked the voice of Rodney Elvis Brown.

Owl gulped and looked up into Rodney's angry face. Measles looked up as well, his face as frightened as Owl's.

Rodney flicked his thumb at Measles. "This is a private conversation, dummy," he said.

Before Measles had a chance to reply, two of Rodney's henchmen grabbed him by the shirt and shoved him down the hallway. Measles looked back once before hurrying off to computer class. There was nothing he could do.

"What do you want, Rodney?" Owl asked, trying to sound braver than he felt.

"Your bones," Rodney sneered. "I want to crush your bones and stuff you in a bag so that I don't have to look at your ugly face anymore."

"But you'll still have to look in the mirror," Owl fired back cheekily, instantly regretting it.

Rodney punched him in the stomach, dropping Owl to his knees and spilling his notebooks onto the floor once again.

"This isn't the place to continue our talk," Rodney hissed down at Owl. "But once school is over, your bones are mine. My old man even knows a good place to dump your sorry carcass."

Rodney laughed as he walked off to class, his cling-ons scurrying behind, each taking turns patting him on the back.

Alone in the hallway, Owl picked up the contents of his notebooks, stuffed them under his arm and hurried to class. Before entering the computer lab, he wiped his eyes, slowed his breathing and tried to look as normal as he could. Then he opened the door and walked inside, his head lowered so he wouldn't have to see the other children staring at him.

At his desk, the message icon was already blinking. Owl launched his chat program and read:

OK?
I wish ...
- Measles

Owl typed back:

I know and thanks.
I'm fine, but after school Rodney says
he's going to grind up my bones and dump the body.
Any ideas?
    - Owl

A few seconds passed.
                Back door won't work,
                Elvis will watch.
                Maybe I do something
                give you time to go.
                - Measles

How?
I don't want you getting hurt, too.
        - Owl

Idea.
Give me few minutes.
        - Measles

OK
        - Owl

Owl tried to concentrate on what the teacher was saying while also trying to imagine what Measles was up to. Every time he glanced back at Measles' desk, he was typing madly away at his keyboard.

Ten minutes passed before the message icon on Owl's desktop began to blink.

            I did it.
            - Measles

Did what?
- Owl

Suddenly, the P.A. system in the classroom crackled to life and the familiar squawky voice of the school secretary came over the airwaves.

"Just a few quick announcements before the school day ends, children," said the voice of Mrs. Pendergrass.

Everyone in the classroom groaned; they hated being called children.

Mrs. Pendergrass went on to mention that a school dance was being organized for the last Friday of the month and that volunteers were needed to decorate the gymnasium. She also mentioned the debate team was having its organizational meeting in room 222 at 3:15 p.m. Then came the surprise:

"And lastly, would Rodney Brown come to the principal's office directly after class. That's Rodney Brown. Thank you."

The airwaves went silent for a moment before the teacher continued his lecture on the necessity of DOS, an operating system that in Owl's opinion should be in the same obsolete category as Latin.

Owl typed on his keyboard:
How did you manage that?
- Owl

Easy.
I fake message to office computer.
Add name to PA list.
- Measles

You're a genius!
- Owl

No one ever say that!
Computer make me smarter.
They not guard back door now.
Not without Rodney.
- Measles

So what's the plan?
- Owl

When class over, you go back door.
I grab bike and meet 1/2way.
Rodney get out school, you long gone.
- Measles

Sounds great.
Thanks again, Measles.
- Owl

OK.
Friend?
- Measles

Owl smiled to himself. It felt great to have a friend — a real friend. He hadn't noticed that Measles had twice ended their chat with a question. Later, he would wish he had answered this one right away. He looked at the clock on the menubar of his computer screen. The school bell was about to ring.

(2)

The plan went without a hitch. Measles had been right. Without Rodney to lead them, the cling-ons were like mindless drones and the back door was left unguarded. Before Rodney was even out the front doors, Owl was pedalling down the gravel road and across empty fields heading to the town dump. Now that one crisis was over, Owl had to meet with the toylings' War Council to see what could be done about the other.

(3)

Inside the War Council's tent, Owl sat before Teddy, listening intently as the toylings discussed their options.

"Owl should go straight to the authorities," said one action figure, a round-bellied, four-inch-tall plastic clown with a rather scary grin.

Teddy looked down at Owl who was sitting cross-legged on the bare dirt floor. "What do you think, Owl?"

Owl shrugged before shyly saying, "I don't think the police or town council would listen to me. I'm a kid. They wouldn't hear a word I said."

Teddy nodded. "Adults have a tendency to dismiss the warnings of children." His one good eye stared directly into Owl's. "How do we convince them this threat is real?"

Owl thought for a moment while the other toys huddled together and talked in quiet whispers. Suddenly, he had an idea.

"I've got it," he announced.

All eyes turned towards him.

"Go on," said Teddy. "We're listening."

Owl began: "If the authorities believe the message is coming from another adult, they'll have to listen. Especially if the warning comes from an environmental group."

"What do you suggest?" Teddy asked.

"I have a friend--"

Teddy cut him off with a wave of his paw. "We can't involve any more humans. We're at risk as it is."

"I don't have to tell him about you," Owl continued. "If I show him the dump site where the barrels are, I'm sure he would help."

Teddy didn't look comfortable, but he told Owl to continue.

"Well, this friend of mine is a computer genius. His name is Measles and I'm positive that with some help he can find his way through the proper channels to make sure the adults listen."

Teddy looked around the room at all the toylings staring back at him.

He lowered his gaze back to Owl. "If you could wait outside while we discuss this matter, we'll come to a decision."

Owl nodded, got to his feet and pushed through the heavy canvas flap. Outside the tent, the toyling market was alive with dancing, trading, wrestling and music. Owl had never seen so many toys in one place before. It made him want to get down on his knees and join in the fun, but most of these toys didn't trust humans anymore and Owl knew he wouldn't be welcomed.

Still, when this crisis was over and he was back home in his trailer, he would make sure to dig out some of his older toys and recreate a market of his own imagination. Now that could be a blast.

The flap opened behind him and Joe poked out his head. "Come on inside, Owl," he said. "The council has come to a decision."

Owl slid back into the tent and sat on the floor. Everyone was staring at him in silence. Owl nervously shifted his gaze up to Teddy.

"We believe your plan is sound," said Teddy. "So long as you promise not to reveal to any outsider the knowledge of our existence."

Owl nodded, but Teddy wasn't finished.

"As you are probably aware, the toylings don't have much affection left towards the humans. At the same time, it is difficult for us not to remember the times when we were cared for and played with by our original owners. You are the first human we have contacted since establishing this community. Many of us are frightened about what would happen if our secret was ever revealed. Children, as much as adults, can be cruel to things they don't understand or that seem different."

Teddy paused and tried to smile.

"Joe assures us that you yourself have felt the pain inflicted by such children and as such would never betray us. We trust Joe's instincts, and over the short time that we have come to know you, we believe our secret will be safe."

Teddy looked around at the group, collecting their nods of agreement as encouragement to continue.

"So contact this friend of yours, take him to the dumping site and try to stop it. Our fate now rests in your hands."

Owl nodded and stood up. "I won't let you down," he said and walked out of the tent.

After stopping at home for a quick supper of macaroni and cheese with chunks of boiled hotdogs mixed in, Owl kissed his mom on the cheek and ran outside to his bike. It wasn't until he was pedalling down the gravel road towards town that he suddenly realized he didn't have a clue where Measles lived. And not only that, he didn't even know Measles' real name.

He braked to a halt, panic filling him. What could he do? He didn't want to wait until school the next day. He wanted to show Measles the dump site tonight and he only had a short time before the sun began to set and the trucks returned to unload more barrels.

"Think, Owl, think," he told himself.

Then an idea dawned on him and he began to pedal faster than before. He had to make it to town before the public library closed.

Screeching to a halt in front of the library, Owl dropped his bike on its side and ran inside. The librarian looked at him over a pair of half-moon glasses. She was much younger and prettier than Owl had been expecting.

"H-h-hi," he mumbled as he slid past her desk and made a beeline for the four computers sitting on a tall table in the middle of the reading area. He had half an hour before the library closed its doors.

Since Owl had never owned a computer of his own, he wasn't exactly a techno-geek. The computer lab at school had shown him the basics, but it was obvious the teacher didn't understand the fascination kids had with the machines. Luckily, Owl had perked up his ears to listen every time one of the other students tried to give the teacher advice on how to make the class more interesting.

Owl pulled up a stool in front of the lone Macintosh, (a computer he found easier to operate, although most of the other kids had PCs at home because it could play more games), and double-clicked the mouse on the Internet icon.

Strange sounds like a mechanical mouse with a stomachache came through the speaker and the internal modem connected to the library's World Wide Web connection. At the same instant, the web browser launched and Owl clicked on the Net Search button.

Now came the tough part. Owl tried to remember what the students had said about finding messages posted by their friends. It was a strange word like a magician would use. It wasn't abracadabra. He pressed his fingers into the side of his head and then it came to him: the word sounded like Deja Vu.

Quickly he typed DejaNews into the search engine and after a few more clicks arrived at the DejaNews site which was designed to search out newsgroup postings by name, subject or e-mail address. Owl crossed his fingers that Measles' on-line identity was the same as his nickname. He typed the name Measles and clicked the search button.

A few seconds later, pages of Measles' postings to groups like *rec.toys.action-figures.discuss*, *alt.hackers* and *comp.sys.ibm.pc.games.action* scrolled past. Owl recognized Measles' language with its proliferation of missing words. He figured those people reading his messages must think it was a form of Internet shorthand. After all, Measles only seemed to leave out words that didn't really matter anyway. Owl grinned as he double-clicked one of the postings about collecting the latest Star Wars toys. He was rewarded with Measles' e-mail address highlighted in blue at the top of the message.

Quickly, Owl hit the reply button, typed a message and sent it. Now he just had to hope that Measles was surfing the 'Net and would get the message in time.

It took less than five minutes before the mail icon in the upper corner of the screen began to blink. Owl crossed his fingers again and brought the mail program to the front.

Hey, Owl.
Where you?
Library?
- Measles

Owl typed a reply and hit send.

Yeah. I need to see you right away,
but I don't know where you live.
- Owl

How find me?
- Measles

DejaNews. It was pretty simple.
- Owl

LOL ;-)
You hacker like me!
- Measles

LOL?
- Owl

Laughing Out Loud.
Want to come my house?
- Measles

Could you meet me at the town dump?
- Owl

The dump? When?
- Measles

Now.
- Owl

On my way. See you.
- Measles

Owl quickly erased all the electronic messages, logged off the 'Net and ran outside. Once astride his bike, he began to pedal like crazy.

(2)

Halfway to the dump, a dark green mountain bike with fat tires pulled up beside Owl. It was Measles.

"Where did you come from?" Owl asked, still pedalling.

"My house," replied Measles, pointing to a small acreage with a pretty yellow house and a huge green lawn. Behind the house was a small grove of trees and high in the branches of an old poplar, Owl could make out the distinct shape of a cool-looking tree house.

Measles continued: "I guessed you come this way. What's rush?"

"We have to get to the dump before dark," said Owl, wrestling his eyes away from Measles face just like hundreds of others had torn their eyes from his. "I need to show you something and then I'll need to ask for a favor."

"No problem," Measles replied, his legs churning as fast as they could as he tried to keep up to Owl. "One question?"

"What?"

"Slow down? Hard to breathe."

"Sorry," Owl blurted, lifting his feet off the pedals to allow his bike to coast.

"It's OK," Measles said. "It's part of Down Syndrome. Sometimes short of breath."

"I'm amazed you can go to regular school," Owl said.

"Why not?" Measles replied hesitantly and a bit coldly. "Lot of people don't think kids like me smart. Because of how talk and look. I lucky. Got great parents! My best friend is computer. It helps me. When online, people don't know I'm different. Fool everyone cause I can hack. I type better than talk. What about you?"

Owl shrugged. "People always seem surprised when I open my mouth and something intelligent comes out. Just because I look different, they assume my brain must be different, too."

"Your brain is different, Owl," Measles said. "You smart."

Owl grinned and began to peddle again. Only this time at a slower pace.

Ten minutes later they were cycling through the town dump towards the hill that looked down on the toxic dumping site. The sun was just sliding behind the hills on the far side of the valley and the sky was turning a deep shade of purple.

"Let's leave our bikes here," Owl said as they reached

the bottom of the small hill.

Measles agreed and together they climbed the hill and lay down on the ground beside the old refrigerator.

"What we looking for?" asked Measles.

"Wait and see," replied Owl.

As soon as the last remaining traces of daylight sank below the horizon, both boys heard a heavy rumble approaching from the north.

"What that?" Measles asked.

"It's what we came to see," Owl replied. "We better keep out of sight."

Soon the rumbling grew louder and the odd twinkles of red and yellow began to approach from the other side of the valley.

"UFO?" whispered Measles.

Owl shook his head and pointed as the twinkles grew into the lights of a half-dozen large trucks. The trucks stopped directly below Owl and Measles' lookout post and two men jumped out of each vehicle.

As the men began to unload the heavy, metal barrels, Owl explained to Measles his plan about contacting environmental groups because he believed the barrels contained illegal toxic waste. He also added that because the barrels weren't sealed properly they could contaminate the town land and poison the water supply.

"Sure it's poison?" Measles asked.

Owl had to agree that he wasn't. Then he came up with an idea. "You stay here," he said. "I'll climb down and see if I can read the warning stickers on the sides of the barrels."

Measles agreed. "Find what's inside, then I search Internet. See if toxic. No point police if only dump old milkshakes."

With a determined grit of his teeth, Owl slid over the top of the hill and began searching for a path down to the bottom of the deep valley.

(3)

Hidden out of sight inside a large coffee can nearby, Joe watched Owl's descent with a nagging sense of dread.

By the time Owl reached the valley floor, he was covered from head to toe in black mud. At least now he blended in so well with the surrounding landscape that none of the workers had spotted him.

Being careful to remain out of sight, Owl made his way to the cavern entrance. The cave looked as though it had been hurriedly scooped out of the side of the hill with a large backhoe. The walls were rough and crumbling, the entrance was jagged and barely supported by thick wooden beams, and the ceiling looked ready to collapse at the slightest sneeze. Obviously, once the men had finished dumping all their illegal waste, they planned to knock away the roof supports and bury the evidence under a ton of dirt.

Owl squeezed himself deeper into the shadows as two workers strolled out of the cave. They were laughing at a joke one of them had made and passed within an arm's length of Owl without seeing him. They looked like space aliens inside their dark green overalls, bright yellow gas masks and bulging eye-protecting goggles.

Owl suddenly wondered if this had been such a smart idea. He hadn't thought to wear any protective clothing.

Before he lost his courage, Owl took a deep breath and ducked through the entrance to the cavern. Quickly and quietly, he began searching for the barrels, his only illumination coming from a half dozen, oil-burning lanterns that dangled from the wooden beams. The beams seemed to be protesting the weight of the hillside with moans, groans and the tiny crackles of snapping fibres.

The sound combined with the eerie light to stir Owl's imagination into believing ghostly voices were warning him to run away. Owl fought back his rising fear and continued deeper into the darkness.

Soon he came across row upon row of barrels being stored at the rear of the cavern. There must have been almost a hundred metal containers and the toxic stench was unbearable.

His eyes stinging from the fumes, Owl readjusted his glasses and peered down at the labels. One warned the contents would burn away skin, another warned the fumes could damage your lungs, two more glowed with the pie-shaped symbol for radioactivity, but none of them said what the barrels actually contained.

Still trying not to breathe through his nose, Owl moved on to the next barrel. The stickers were practically identical, except Owl noticed a few additions like the symbol of the hand dissolving into a skeleton that meant corrosive and there was another symbol for poison.

Owl may not have learned exactly what was inside the barrels, but at least now he could tell it was far more dangerous than a small town dump normally allowed.

Without warning, a heavy footstep crunched behind him. Instantly alert, Owl swiveled on his heels to dart away. But before he could get his feet to move forward, a heavy, gloved hand clamped over his mouth and his arms were pinned firmly to his sides.

Owl tried to wriggle free, but it was no use.

"What have we here?" growled a man's angry voice into Owl's ear. "A little rat lost in the dump?"

Owl was spun around to face the grinning mug of the man from the black pickup truck.

"Who are you and why are you sneaking around?" the man demanded.

"I-I-I was just out for a walk," Owl stuttered.

"Don't lie to me, boy," the man barked. In the gloomy lantern light of the cavern, he looked even more like rotten Rodney than he had from a distance. The same prominent cheekbones, dark eyes and thick, jet-black hair.

"I wouldn't lie," Owl lied. "You're Rodney's dad, right?"

"You know my boy?" the man asked, puzzled.

"S-s-sure, we go to the same school together."

"Then you should know better than to poke your nose into other people's affairs."

Before Owl could reply, he felt himself being thrown into the grasp of two workmen. They held his arms so tightly, pinching the tender wing-like skin beneath, Owl thought they were going to snap them off.

"What do you want us to do with him, Frank?" asked one of the workmen. His voice sounded like Darth Vader as it hissed through the yellow gas mask.

Owl heard a horrible ripping sound and almost peed his pants.

"Just hold him steady," replied Frank as he advanced on Owl.

The ripping sound had been the opening of a new spool of industrial-strength duct tape. Soon, Owl found his arms, ankles and wrists bound tight by coils of the tape. When Frank was finished, Owl looked like a modern-day mummy wrapped in grey plastic instead of white bandages.

"We can't just leave him here," protested the other workman.

"Sure we can," replied Frank. "We only have another day before we're finished. Then we can bury him with the

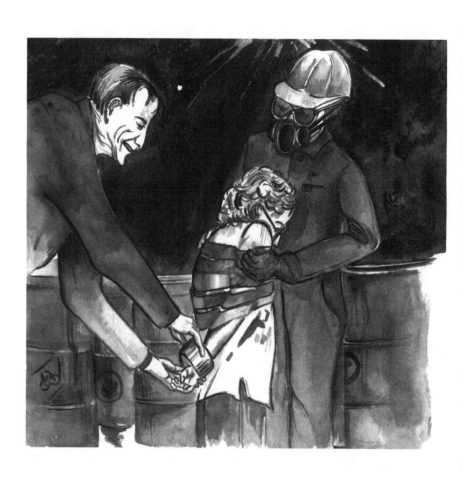

rest of the evidence."

Owl couldn't believe what he was hearing. They were going to leave him to die.

"Why are you doing this?" Owl blurted, trying hard to fight back his tears. "What's in these barrels anyway that you have to bury them at night?"

"What isn't in them?" Frank answered casually. "The names don't mean much to me. PCBs, waste oil, fly ash, waste acid, shredder dust, who cares? All I know is that people pay big bucks to get rid of the stuff."

"But aren't you worried about what it'll do to the land and the water?" asked Owl, struggling to think of a plan of escape but coming up empty.

"Nah," Frank said with a shake of his head. "By the time this stuff leaks into the soil, I'll be long gone. It's your problem, boy, but I wouldn't worry about it. You won't be around for too much longer either."

"People will miss me," Owl piped up. "They'll come looking."

Frank laughed. "Nobody will find you here, boy. Especially with the entrance sealed up."

"But you can't just leave me here," Owl protested.

"I can do whatever I want, boy," Frank laughed again. "Soon I'm going to be a very rich man. Heck, I might even buy this town and turn this little dump into a real profit-making machine."

Laughing to himself as he walked out of the cavern, Frank paused at the cave entrance and gave the support beam a swift kick. As he quickly ran into the clearing, the mouth of the cavern began to collapse.

Inside, Owl felt like the entire hillside was coming down on top of him. He tried to scream, but had to close his mouth and shut his eyes as the cavern filled with dirt, dust, rocks and an avalanche of mud.

Outside, standing safely beside his truck, Frank looked back at the avalanche that had sealed the cave and grinned.

"We'll need to remember and bring the backhoe with us tomorrow night," he said to the remaining two workers. "It looks like we'll have to do a little digging."

(2)

It took a long time for the roaring in Owl's ears to calm down and for the taste of dirt to leave his mouth. He was buried almost up to his neck in a thin blanket of loose dirt. With his hands bound tight to his waist, he had no way to dig himself free.

Salty tracks began to stream down his muddy face.

(3)

At the lookout above, Measles felt the blood drain from his face when he saw the cavern entrance collapse. He had watched Owl sneak inside, but hadn't seen him come back out.

As soon as the trucks drove away, Measles began searching for a path down to the valley floor. It was difficult to see as the sun had sunk below the hills and the moon was barely a sliver in the night sky, but Measles was determined to help his friend.

Just a short distance away, Joe was already rappelling down the side of the valley wall on a rope he had secured to the rusted bulk of an old wheel axle. His first instinct had been to report back to the War Council, but he knew from suffocating experience how quickly oxygen could get used up inside a cramped area.

Owl needed his help and he needed it fast.

(4)

Inside the dark cavern, Owl was finding it difficult to breathe. The putrid air was clogged with dust and an acrid stench that rose from a green-grey mass oozing out of ruptures in the sides of the barrels.

Owl suddenly realized that he didn't want to die. It was something he had never thought about before. Despite his handicaps, none of them were life threatening so he had never had to face the concept of death before.

He knew people died, of course, he had seen it on television, but he had never really thought that it might happen to him one day. He definitely had never imagined that he would die buried up to his neck in dirt while an oozing, radioactive puddle threatened to dissolve his flesh and bones for a midnight snack.

He was beginning to panic and he knew that was the one thing you should never do in a crisis situation. He tried to calm himself. "What would John Wayne or Schwarzenegger do?" he asked himself. The answer wasn't very encouraging: "Schwarzenegger would rip off the duct tape and tear through the caved-in entrance like it was butter. And John Wayne wouldn't have been captured in the first place."

So the only real question he could ask was: "What do *I* do?"

He had no answers.

(5)

Joe unclipped himself from the climbing rope and scrambled over the rocks to the landslide that sealed the entrance to the cavern.

The rocks and mud were jammed tight together and there didn't seem to be any gaps that would allow him or even air inside. Quickly, he slipped off his backpack and rummaged inside. All he had was a standard plastic bayonet, two wooden matches, a firecracker that he had salvaged from a box of soggy discards and packed tight with extra gunpowder, and a collapsible plastic shovel.

He had no time to waste.

Using the bayonet, he loosened a few stones to give the shovel some room to bite in. Then he dug as deep a hole as he could manage, slipped in the firecracker, lit the fuse and dived for cover.

The noise was deafening.

Halfway up the valley wall, Measles heard the loud pop and thought a guard, who must have been left behind to protect the cavern, was shooting at him. Inside the cavern, Owl thought an earthquake was about to bring the rest of the roof down on top of him.

Even Joe was staggered by the noise, but he wasted no time in rushing to the deep hole and building up support beams of splintered wood and stone to keep the gopher-sized tunnel from collapsing again. Once he had the walls and ceiling secured, Joe pulled out his shovel and began to dig again. It only took a few more minutes before he broke through the other side.

"Owl!" Joe called out as he wriggled his shoulders through the opening and dropped to the dirt floor. "Are you okay?"

Owl gasped at the sound. "Joe is that you?"

"Hey, who else were you expecting — the tooth fairy?" Joe laughed, relieved to hear his friend's voice.

"Untie me will you, I thought I was going to die."

"Nobody dies on my watch, pal," the toyling said as he ran to where Owl was half buried in dirt.

Joe scrambled around the blanket of dirt and was relieved to see there was enough room between Owl and the cavern wall to reach the tape that bound Owl's wrists. Joe began to cut through the duct tape with his knife, but the tape was far too sticky to allow for any leverage.

"I'll need to get something sharper," Joe said in frustration. "Any ideas?"

"Where's Measles?" Owl asked. "Maybe he has a pocketknife."

"He was climbing down the hill and will probably be here soon, but I can't show myself to him and there's no way he'd be able to get inside."

"I trust him, Joe," Owl said pleadingly. "You can too."

"I'm sure I can, but I'm under strict orders," Joe said apologetically. "If it was just my safety to be concerned about, I'd let him see me no problem. But I have to look after the interests of the whole village. Sorry, buddy, I just can't risk it."

Owl nodded his understanding, and then he had an idea.

"Maybe you don't have to show yourself," he said. "We just need to get Measles to notice the tunnel you built. If I can talk to him, maybe I can get him to throw his knife or at least something sharp inside."

"Good idea. What do we do?" asked Joe.

"Can you make a flag - something that will catch his eye?"

Joe looked down at the handle of his shovel and then ripped off his shirt, exposing the stump of his missing arm. "One flag coming up."

CHAPTER 7
NO ESCAPE

With bruised knees and skinned elbows, Measles managed to scramble, slide and fall down the muddy slope. When his feet finally landed on the valley floor, he paused for a moment to wipe the sweat from his brow and check that he wasn't missing any of his limbs.

He groaned when he saw the state of his clothes, but quickly put aside worries of what his mom would say when he saw the blocked entrance to the cavern.

"Owl!" he screamed, running to where the entrance should have been to begin searching for a way inside. It looked useless; the whole entrance was filled with mud, clay, rocks and hunks of railway line timber.

"Owl!" he yelled again, trying to make his voice pierce the mud barrier. "Owl! You in there?"

He waited a moment, trying to figure out what to do, when he heard a muffled reply. It was Owl — he was still alive.

Measles looked around the valley floor in search of a shovel or anything that would help him dig, but he came up empty. That was when he noticed a strange flag sticking out of the mud on a lower part of the landslide.

The flag looked to be made from a doll-sized, mud-stained shirt and a tiny plastic shovel. Measles bent down for a closer look and found he could suddenly hear Owl's voice much clearer.

"I hear you Owl," Measles called into the small tunnel. "The men left air hole. Marked it with flag."

"Measles!" Owl yelled to make sure he would be heard. "Do you have a knife?"

Measles dug into his pocket and pulled out a small, red Swiss Army knife with two blades. "Yeah. It's just little though."

"Great!" Owl yelled back. "Can you throw it down the tunnel. Throw it as hard as you can."

"You reach?" Measles called.

"It'll help me get free," Owl called back, not wanting to lie to his friend.

"OK," Measles yelled before aiming for the tunnel entrance and throwing the knife deep inside. "You reach?"

"Hold on," Owl called back as Joe ran to the tunnel and retrieved the knife. "I've got it!" Owl yelled.

Holding the small metal blade in both hands, Joe quickly sliced through the duct tape that bound Owl's wrists and arms. Once Owl could move his arms again, he dug himself out of the mud and took the knife off Joe to cut the tape around his ankles.

Finally, he was able to move away from the expanding puddle of smelly slime that still oozed from the broken barrels, and press his mouth against the cool air of the tiny tunnel that Joe had made.

"Thanks, Measles," he called through the tunnel, still gulping lungfuls of air. "They had me tied up in here and the stench coming from the barrels is awful."

Measles sighed with relief. "I'm glad you OK. When I saw the entrance . . . I didn't know . . . ."

"Yeah, it was pretty scary," Owl agreed. "And you'll never guess who's in charge of these polluters."

"Who?" Measles asked.

"Rodney's dad."

"Elvis!" Measles gasped. "You kidding me."

"Nope, I saw his face up close and personal."

"Ah, geez. What we to do?"

"I'm not sure," Owl said, scratching his head. "Is there any way to dig me out of here?"

"Nope. I don't think," answered Measles. "I've looked for a shovel, nothing. I can get help though. My dad has Bobcat."

"Yeah, maybe . . ." Owl paused as he looked down at Joe who was sitting on a rock by his elbow. "No, wait."

"For?" Measles asked. "You don't want to be trapped. They'll come back."

"No, I don't want to be trapped," Owl had to agree, "but if you get help now, we'll never be able to prove that Rodney's dad is the one dumping all this toxic stuff. He'll deny the whole thing, and who's going to believe a couple of ten-year-olds?"

Measles sat down on the dirt, dejected.

"You right," he said. "The adults won't listen to us."

"But," continued Owl, "if you can get the adults to show up tomorrow night when Rodney's dad and his men are dumping more barrels . . ."

"Yeah," Measles piped in. "Then they must believe. But what you? Your mom will worry."

"I'll need to stay here," Owl said with a grimace. "But are you sure you can get the police and the environmentalists to show up tomorrow night?"

"I'll work the 'Net soon as I home," Measles said. "Did you find what in barrels?"

"Not specifically, although Rodney's dad listed off stuff like PCBs, waste oil, fly ash, waste acid and shredder dust. Will that do?"

"I don't know," Measles said, feeling a wave of anxiety churn in his stomach. "Tough to remember."

"Hold on," Owl called to Measles.

He turned to Joe, lowered his voice, and asked: "Can you remove some of the warning labels from the barrels and pass them to Measles?"

Joe grinned and began scaling the mud wall like a spider. Or a trained Navy Seal, Owl thought.

"What you doing?" Measles called.

"Getting you a note with some of the names on it."

Measles grinned, feeling his anxiety ease. "That's good," he called.

After a few minutes, Joe returned with scraps of sticky paper and warning labels.

"Reach into the hole," Owl called out to Measles. "I'll try and pass them to you."

"OK," Measles called back as he lay down on the muddy ground and stuck his arm deep into the hole.

Joe crawled forward from his end and stuffed the papers into Measles hand.

"Got it," Measles cried, pulling the sticky mess out of the hole.

"Great," Owl called out. "Will it help?"

"I'll do my best," answered Measles, still sounding hesitant.

"When you do the search," Owl piped in helpfully, "look for names that mention environment and protection. Greenpeace might be able to help, too, but I don't know if they have a local chapter."

"OK. Trust me?" Measles asked.

"Hey, if you can't do it," Owl said, trying to sound braver than he felt, "no one can."

Measles looked down into the tiny tunnel again, a look of concern furrowing his freckled brow. "Sure you going be okay?"

"Well, I've slept in better places . . .," Owl paused and looked down at Joe, who flashed him the thumbs-up sign. "But I'll be fine."

"See tomorrow then," Measles said, getting to his feet and looking at the long climb back up the muddy hill he still had to make.

"Don't be late," Owl called after him, adding quickly, "Friend," but Measles was already gone.

(2)

"What's the plan now, Joe?" Owl asked as he sat down in the dirt, his eyes focused nervously on the ever-expanding puddle of green-grey ooze that bubbled out of the barrels at the rear of the cavern.

Joe had disappeared into the tiny tunnel, returning quickly with his muddy shirt and shovel.

"I'll need to meet with the War Council," Joe replied, slipping on his shirt and repacking his backpack. "We can't leave you here to face the polluters alone. Your friend might not make it back."

"Oh, he'll be back," Owl said reassuringly. "I just hope he can convince the adults to return with him."

"Exactly," Joe said with a grimace. "We'll need to prepare for the worst and hope for the best."

Owl smiled. "That sounds like something the Duke would say."

"The Duke?" Joe asked.

"You know, John Wayne."

"Don't know him," Joe said.

"You don't know John Wayne?" Owl asked incredulously. "His movies are on TV all the time."

"We don't have TV in the village," Joe said. "It's tough

to get electricity."

Owl thought about that for a moment. "Well, when this is all over, you'll need to come to my house one night when my mom's out and we'll watch a John Wayne marathon. Maybe even throw in a Schwarzenegger and a Stallone. How does that sound?"

Joe grinned. "Sounds like fun."

The soldier readjusted the backpack on his shoulders, secured his plastic knife to a sheath on his leg and pinned the loose sleeve of his missing arm to his chest.

"I have to go," he said. "The War Council will be waiting for my report and there's a lot of planning to do before tomorrow night."

Owl nodded, his eyes focusing on the growing puddle of smelly ooze.

"You will come back, right?" he asked.

"As soon as I can," Joe replied, heading for the tunnel. "Don't worry, you won't face this alone."

"Well," Owl sighed, settling his back against a large boulder. "You know where to find me."

Joe flashed Owl a quick salute and disappeared into the tunnel.

Alone in the flickering light of two oil-burning lanterns, Owl felt like crying, but this time he knew he couldn't. There was a war coming and he had to steel himself to be braver than he had ever been before.

With one eye on the encroaching toxic ooze, he tried to get some sleep.

CHAPTER 8
WAR COUNCIL

Joe's return sent the toyling village into a flurry of activity. Silent crowds gathered outside the War Council's tent, waiting on word from the toylings inside. But as the meeting dragged on, the crowd became restless. It wasn't in their nature to waste time worrying. Every one of them had been through a hurtful event that had changed them from toy to toyling. And as such, they now believed in the philosophy of *carpe diem* (seize the day) to enjoy every moment.

Soon the gathered throng lit several warming fires and began to sing songs and tell stories, and before you knew it the market became so alive with dancing and merriment that any stranger would swear it was a harvest festival.

"What is all that noise out there?" Teddy asked as he surveyed the concerned faces of the council members inside the tent.

Joe poked his head outside the tent flap and quickly ducked back inside.

"It looks like a party," he said with a grin. "Everyone is probably worried that we're going to be discovered. They're holding a party to distract themselves."

"Maybe they have a right to be worried," Teddy said, folding his arms across his belly. "If we're going to help Owl, we might not have any choice but to reveal ourselves - and if we did that . . ." Teddy allowed his voice to trail off into silence.

The other council members began to nod their heads and Joe could feel a twinge of panic building in his belly as he realized that his promise to Owl might be broken.

"Owl has put his own life at risk to help us," Joe said, breaking the silence. "I know he wouldn't want us to risk the village, but all I need is a strike team of volunteers to help him."

Joe continued without waiting for a response. "If we do nothing, the village will be destroyed by pollution."

A large stuffed penguin with greying temples jumped to his feet, waving one of his flippers to get everyone's attention. "Don't forget it was the humans who started this," he squawked. "We didn't pollute the land."

"Neither did Owl," Joe fired back. "The only reason he's buried in that cave is because we asked him to help."

"But if you are captured," interrupted Teddy. "Think what the humans would do to us then."

Joe stared unflinchingly into Teddy's eyes. "If captured, the humans would never know my team was anything but a bunch of harmless toys."

"You don't mean--," Teddy gasped. "We can't ask you to do that."

"You're not asking," Joe replied calmly. "I'm volunteering. And I vow that if I am captured I will give up being a toyling."

The whole council erupted with a dozen different voices trying to speak at once. Everyone knew that as a toyling they had the ability to switch back to being an unthinking and unfeeling piece of plastic. With a simple thought, they could give up the miraculous existence that had been given to them. But in all the years of the village, no one had ever chosen to return to being merely a toy.

"And," Joe continued, speaking louder to be heard over the noise, "I will ask every volunteer on my strike team to make the same promise to this council. If we are captured, the existence of the village will be protected."

"Who would volunteer for such a thing?" squawked the stuffed penguin.

"I volunteer," said a brightly colored, eight-inch-tall Manga warrior as it rose to its feet. The fierce toyling was a comic-book blend of Samurai warrior, insect and robot.

Joe looked over and felt one eyebrow arch in surprise as the warrior removed its helmet to reveal a startlingly beautiful Asian woman with flowing raven-black hair. Joe cracked a rare smile. He hadn't known the formidable warrior's armor concealed such a lovely woman.

"Count us in, too," came the cry from Mik and his three long-legged brothers.

"You're not going anywhere without us, Joe," declared a squad of six rubber wrestlers.

"That makes twelve," Joe said. "I think that'll be enough."

Teddy silenced the crowd with a wave of his arms. "Do the volunteers know what they are risking in this venture?" he asked sternly.

All the volunteers nodded.

"Then the council has no choice but to wish you all the best of luck and hope that your mission is a success." Teddy paused, allowing his words to sink in. "Our fate and the future of this village is in your hands."

Joe beckoned to the volunteers. "We've got a lot of planning to do," he said. "We better get to it."

And with those words, the twelve volunteers exited the tent.

(2)

Inside his darkened bedroom, Measles typed madly on the keyboard of his computer.

He started by doing an Internet search for "enviromint". As hard as he was trying, as hard as he was thinking, he still had to spell the word three different times before getting one the computer hit on. Even then, the web site the computer link took him to didn't seem to have anything to do with the environment.

Finally, he went to another program, the one he wrote all his school reports in, and spell checked all the words he thought he'd need. "Enviromint" became "environment" and "protactshun" became "protection".

"Glad computer can do what I can't," Measles said to himself, patting the beige box as another kid might pet a dog or cat. His head began to hurt from the strain, but Measles reminded himself he had another friend now, and that friend was in trouble. He returned to the Internet search engine.

For the word "environment", the search engine returned 8,944,478 documents that matched his query. The amount of information out there was incredible, but it was also too much for him to sort through in order to find the right people who would respond to his request for help.

He narrowed his search to "environment + protection" and this time the search engine returned 4,807,460 documents. It was still too much information.

"OK, you want play rough?" Measles asked the computer as he began to refine his search once more.

It took a long time, but by using the information printed on the stickers Owl had given him, and the spell-checked word list he had made, he finally tracked down the e-mail addresses for the Environmental Protection Agency, Greenpeace, Surfers Against Sewage and a half-dozen other groups who looked like they might be able to

help. And just to make sure, he posted a call for help on all the environmental newsgroups he could find. Now he just had to hope that somebody listened before it was too late.

(3)

Armed with ropes, elastic bands, firecrackers and backpacks filled with glass marbles, Joe led his motley crew of volunteers down the steep valley wall to the small tunnel that led into the sealed cavern.

Inside, Joe found Owl fast asleep against a large boulder. The puddle of toxic ooze had grown considerably since he had left, but it was still at least four feet away from Owl's outstretched feet.

"Okay, men," he said in a whisper. The Manga warrior made a slight shuffling sound with her feet, but it was enough to make Joe quickly add, "And women," before continuing with his speech. "The enemy is faster, larger and better armed. Our main objective is to make sure Owl isn't harmed and that he gets to safety once the humans remove the rubble blocking the entrance. Our secondary objective is not to be discovered."

Joe waved his arms around the cavern. "We'll use the shadows and high ledges to hide ourselves and we'll only engage the enemy if forced to. I don't want anyone taking needless risks. Is that clear?"

The team of volunteers nodded as one.

"Now this is your last chance to walk away," Joe continued. "If any one of you no longer wants to see this mission through, you can leave now."

Joe studied each of the volunteers' faces, but nobody backed down.

Satisfied with his team, Joe allowed a rare smile to cross

his face. "Good, now take your places as high up on the walls as you can and try to get some rest. It's going to be a busy day tomorrow."

As the volunteers scaled the walls and made their beds on ledges and inside small burrows and caves, Joe rested his back on the same boulder as Owl, tilted his plastic cap over his eyes and pretended to go to sleep.

He knew his team would never relax if they thought he was still awake, but at the same time he needed to keep at least one eye on the expanding toxic puddle.

The moment the bedside alarm clock began its daily buzz, Measles was out of bed and shaking the mouse to bring his computer out of sleep mode.

Once the monitor warmed up, Measles logged onto his Internet provider and downloaded his e-mail. There were five pieces of SPAM (mass-mailed electronic junk mail, which he deleted without reading), two requests from other students wanting help with a computer class assignment, (Measles sent them a copy of his usual freelance rates consisting of Star Wars, X-Men and Spawn action figures that he didn't already own), and one from his Aunt Netta in Scotland that was to be printed out for his mom.

That was it.

There was no response from the Environmental Protection Agency or Greenpeace or a reply to any of his newsgroup postings. Nothing.

Not believing his eyes, he checked his mail again, but there were no new messages.

"Graham!" called the voice of his mom from the kitchen. "Are you on the Net again? I need to make a phone call."

Measles sighed and logged off.

"Off now, mom," Measles called back. "Go ahead."

"Thanks, Sweetie. Now wash up and come down for breakfast."

Measles plodded dejectedly into the bathroom, washed his face, combed his hair and dressed in his usual outfit of jeans and a clean T-shirt. His mom was still on the phone when he entered the kitchen and sat down to a bowl of

Rice Krispies and toast with peanut butter and cheese singles.

After breakfast, he ran back upstairs, fired up his modem and checked his e-mail again. His only reward was another unwelcome piece of SPAM. He quickly added the sender's address to his filter list and forwarded a copy to the President of the United States. He figured that since most spammers were based in America, if the White House received enough of the annoying messages they might do something to stop it. After all, in this age of electronic communication there should be a law against privacy pollution.

"Graham!" called his mom again. "You'll be late for school."

"I'm going, I'm going," Measles called back as he stuffed his homework in his backpack.

With one last glance at his empty e-mail Inbox, Measles ran downstairs and jumped on his bike. He hoped inspiration would strike before the end of the day - Owl's life depended on it.

(2)

"OK, team," Joe called as a beam of warm sunlight shone like a torch through the tiny tunnel in the otherwise dark and musty cavern. "Our first job is to stop that toxic ooze from creeping any closer to Owl."

At the mention of his name, Owl yawned and rubbed at his eyes. "Whas goin' on," he mumbled sleepily.

"The reinforcements are here," Joe said with a grin. "But our toxic puddle over there keeps growing." He pointed at the green lake that was barely two feet away from Owl's shoes.

"How many barrels are punctured?" Owl asked,

reflexively pulling his feet closer to his chest.

"I can't tell from here," the soldier said, "but I think we should dig a trench to stop it from reaching you."

"Good idea," Owl replied. "Let me help."

Soon, Owl and the team of living action figures were scraping a large trench out of the cavern floor with sharp stones plucked from the crumbling walls. The dirt taken out of the trench was used to build a wall on one side to act like a dam in case the trench overflowed. Owl also reinforced the dam with as many large boulders as he could find.

It took almost two hours, but when they were done, Owl felt much safer. After all, he might not know what the ingredients of the toxic ooze were, but he knew from all the warning signs plastered on the barrels that he didn't want to take a bath in it.

"Now what do we do?" Owl asked, looking down at the dirty faces of the twelve-member team.

"Now," Joe said, wiping his brow. "We build a few surprises for our expected guests."

Mik and the rest of the squad grinned. This was going to be the fun stuff.

(3)

Measles had a hard time concentrating on anything his computer lab instructor had to say — and this was his favorite class. Of course, thanks to the special-education programs he had taken for most of his life, he had been working on computers for years before the other "normal" students had. And even though he found today's class on 3D graphics interesting, he just couldn't get his mind off Owl.

He had been so sure that by tracking down the right

organizations on the Net he would have had a full-scale army of environmentalists charging into town by now. Instead, he had zip, nadda, nothing.

The P.A. system in the classroom crackled to life.

"I have an emergency announcement, children," said the voice of Mrs. Pendergrass.

Everyone in the classroom groaned as usual.

"There's a Ms. Hunter here and she reports that her son, Owl, has gone missing. If anyone has seen this child or knows of his whereabouts, please come to the principal's office immediately. I repeat, if there is any student who knows where Owl Hunter is, please come to the principal's office. His mother is very worried."

Measles looked down at his hands. He knew exactly where Owl was, but he couldn't tell the adults. He had made Owl a promise that he wouldn't bring help until nightfall.

Then he had an idea. Quickly, he began typing on his computer, being careful to disguise his identity. When he hit send, a message instantly appeared on Mrs. Pendergrass's computer terminal.

The message read:

Dear Owl's Mom:
Owl OK. Not worry.
Home tonight.
- A Friend

The P.A. system crackled to life again.

"Whoever just sent the message for Ms. Hunter, come to the principal's office at once," demanded Mrs. Pendergrass in a high-pitched squeal. "I don't think it's very funny."

Measles typed another message.

I not meaning funny.
Owl is safe.
Home tonight.
- A Friend

"You little rascal!" squawked Mrs. Pendergrass over the P.A. system. "Come to the principal's office at once."

All the students in the classroom began to laugh.

Then another voice came over the P.A. This one was softer and much more soothing.

"Thank you for the message, friend," said the voice of Owl's mom. "It's difficult not to worry."

Measles typed one last message.

Owl is friend.
He doing important thing.
Home tonight.
- A Friend

The P.A. went silent for a few minutes before the static buzz returned and Mrs. Pendergrass's voice whispered harshly over the airwaves: "I'll find out who you are you little sneak. Don't think you can hide from me."

The whole classroom erupted into laughter and even the teacher had a difficult time keeping the grin off his face.

Before the class ended, Measles double-checked that he had erased all his tracks from the school's system - just in case Mrs. Pendergrass was smarter than she looked.

(4)

After school, Measles ran for his bike. He wanted to get home as soon as possible to see if any of his e-mail had been answered. But just as he climbed into the saddle, two pairs of hands grabbed the handlebars.

"Going somewhere, Measly?" Rodney Elvis Brown asked as two of his henchmen held onto Measles' bike.

"Just home," Measles replied.

"You're not going to meet your boyfriend?" Rodney taunted.

"Boyfriend?"

"The freak, like you."

"You mean Owl?" Measles asked defiantly, his anger burning in his belly.

"No," Rodney sneered, leaning in closer so his stale breath washed over Measles' face. "I mean the freak."

"You only freak here, Rodney," Measles retaliated. At the same instant, he wrenched his bike free from the henchmen's grasp and began to pedal like he had never pedaled before.

"You'll regret that," Rodney screamed after him. "My dad tells me he has a surprise tonight - and it smells like baked Owl."

Measles squeezed hard on the brakes and spun his bike around to face Rodney.

"What you mean?" he asked, feeling his throat tighten with panic.

Rodney grinned menacingly.

"Let's just say that a certain freakish looking snoop seems to have poked its bird-beaked nose in the way of one of my old man's projects."

"Dad tell you that?" Measles asked.

"Not directly, but I overheard a certain discussion when

he thought I was asleep," Rodney jabbed back. "And I don't think anyone will object if I make the freak beg for mercy before my old man buries him alive."

"I wrong, Rodney," Measles called out so that all the passing students could hear. "You not freak."

Rodney grinned proudly, but Measles wasn't finished.

"You a monster," Measles spat, turned his bike around and pedaled for home as fast as he could.

(5)

Safe at home, Measles checked his e-mail.

There were no messages.

CHAPTER 10
KNOCK, KNOCK

Owl was hungry.

It hadn't crossed his mind to ask Measles to bring him anything to eat and now all he could think about was burgers, fries, peanut butter, chicken, spaghetti, sausages, bagels ... he felt himself drool at the images of food dancing in his mind as his stomach grumbled.

"You okay, Owl?" Joe asked as he finished securing another trip wire to a large boulder.

Owl nodded. "I'm just hungry," he said, trying to will his stomach to be quiet.

"We brought along some rations, but they're probably so small you wouldn't even be able to taste them."

"That's okay," Owl said, "it's almost nightfall. Rodney's dad and his goons should be arriving soon."

"We'll be ready," Joe said, sitting down on a rock beside Owl. "You'll be home soon."

Unexpectedly, they heard the crunch of a shovel being forced into dirt. It was followed by the muffled voices of several humans.

Owl strained to listen and heard a boy's voice shout: "Hey, there's an air tunnel down here. He must be able to breathe."

The boy's voice faded away to be replaced by another.

"Hey, freak. You still alive?" asked the voice of Rodney Elvis Brown.

Owl gasped.

"W-w-what are you doing here?" he called back in panic.

Rodney laughed.

"I came to dig you out so we could play a little before my old man buries you."

The laughter of a half-dozen boys cheered Rodney on as they all began to dig into the rubble that blocked the mouth of the cavern.

Owl looked at Joe, his eyes wide with worry. He needed a friend now more than he had ever needed anything, but where was Measles?

"Don't worry," Joe whispered. "This wasn't part of the plan, but we'll handle it."

Dirt and stones began raining down on Owl's head as the boys dug from the outside without any care for his safety. Owl had nowhere to hide. He was trapped between the crumbling rubble and the small lake of toxic ooze.

"Come on, Measles," Owl whispered to himself. "Don't let me down."

(2)

Measles secured his father's cell phone into a zippered pocket of his coat and began pedalling to the town dump. Flying over hills and swerving around piles of trash, he soon arrived at the lookout spot Owl had taken him to the day before. Owl's bike was still lying on its side at the bottom of the small hill.

Measles laid his bike down beside Owl's and scrambled to the top beside the old refrigerator. He was surprised to hear voices down in the valley and was doubly shocked when he saw it was Rodney and his gang. They were armed with shovels and were digging away at the cavern entrance.

Measles looked at his watch. Nightfall was still almost an hour away.

Quickly, he scanned his surroundings and began

gathering up old tin cans. Without hesitation, he packed the tin cans with mud and rocks until he had two dozen of them lined up in front of him. Then he puckered his lips and blew a shrill whistle.

Down below, Rodney and his gang stopped digging and looked up.

Even inside the cavern, Owl heard the whistle.

"What's that?" he asked Joe.

Joe shrugged.

"What's that?" asked one of the cling-ons outside.

Rodney shrugged.

Then came a rain of rock-filled baked bean and cream corn cans. The boys shrieked, dropped their shovels and ran from the cavern entrance as the tin cans slammed into the valley floor. The rusted seams of the cans split open on impact to spray their mucky contents in a wide arc.

"It's Measles!" Rodney cried, pointing to the top of the cliff. "Get him!"

Four of the boys instantly began running for the cliff face, but were stopped as another hailstorm of tin cans crashed to the ground.

"Get up there!" Rodney yelled again.

"But, but," one of the boys sputtered.

"No excuses," Rodney screamed. "I want his head!"

The four boys ran for the cliff face again, but this time the heavy, rock-filled cans hit two of them. Both boys fell to the ground in pain while the other two made it to the cliff and started to climb. The jutting lip of the cliff face above them protected the two climbers, like an umbrella, from any further threat from Measles' barrage.

"Get up you wimps," Rodney commanded the two boys lying on the ground.

One of the boys, his numb arm held tight against his chest, his eyes filling with tears, just shook his head and walked off to get his bike. The other boy, limping with a bruised and charley-horsed leg, joined him.

"Wimps!" Rodney yelled again at their retreating backs.

Both boys ignored him.

Inside the cavern, Owl stared at Joe.

"It's Measles," he said, his face alight with happiness and worry. "I knew he'd make it, but you have to help him."

"We can't show ourselves," Joe replied. "You know that."

"He's our only hope," said Owl. "He's the one calling in the cavalry. And if Rodney's gang gets him, we're all dead meat."

Joe nodded. He knew Owl spoke the truth.

"Okay, gang," he called out. "Stop them from scaling the walls. Protect Measles."

Mik and his three brothers grinned as they vanished into tunnels they had dug near the top of the blocked entrance.

The two climbers were too busy looking for foot and handholds in the cliff face to notice the four tiny faces that stuck out of the dirt just above them.

Mik nodded to his brothers and instantly two of them stretched an elastic band above their heads while the other two loaded a glass marble into the centre of the homemade slingshot and pulled it back.

"Fire!" Mik commanded.

The two boys didn't know what hit them. The bruising impact of the marbles on the knuckles of their hands caused them to release their grip on the cliff face and they

tumbled awkwardly to the valley floor. Neither landing was graceful. All the air was knocked out of their lungs and both boys collapsed on their backs — their fighting spirit crushed.

Before the boys even hit bottom, Mik and his brothers had disappeared back inside the tunnels.

"What happened?" Rodney yelled, running up to them.

"Something hit us," one of the boys groaned, rubbing his sore hand and gulping in air. "Measles must have thrown more cans."

"No, he didn't," Rodney muttered. "I think he's run out of ammo. Get back up there."

Both boys shook their heads at once.

"I think I'm going to be sick," one of them groaned.

"Me, too," said the other as together they staggered to their bikes and pedaled away.

Rodney watched them go before turning to his last two followers.

"You two," he commanded. "Get up there and make that little weasel pay."

(3)

Up above, Measles studied his remaining cache of two tin cans and wondered if he should use them now or hold on for later. By the time he decided to keep them in reserve, it was too late anyway. The boys had reached the cliff face and were beginning to climb.

"There're two more," Joe called out from within the cavern. "Are you ready, Mik?"

Mik flashed a thumbs-up as the wrestlers carefully carried two cans filled with toxic sludge up to the high tunnels.

The two climbers were trying to be cautious as they

scaled the cliff face. But even so they had to concentrate more on finding handholds than they did on what was above them.

Mik checked the position of the two climbers then signaled the wrestlers to get into position.

Once everyone was set, Mik stuck two fingers into the corners of his mouth and blew a loud whistle.

When the climbers looked up to see what the noise was, Mik signaled the wrestlers to dump the toxic ooze.

Both boys screamed and released their grip on the cliff face as the noxious slime fell towards them. They hit the ground with a painful thump and scrambled back quickly as the translucent green slime splashed at their feet, releasing a horrible odor.

"What happened this time?" Rodney screamed as he marched forward.

"Measles dumped cans of gross stuff on us," one of the boys moaned as he nursed a twisted ankle.

"Ib smells lib robben ebbs," mumbled the other boy, who was trying not to cry as blood dripped out of his mouth. He had bitten his tongue when he landed.

"What did he say?" Rodney asked.

"I think he said 'it smells like rotten eggs'," replied the first boy, trying to get to his feet but finding he couldn't put any weight on his sore ankle.

"Well plug your noses and get back up there," Rodney commanded.

Both boys shook their heads.

"We gobba bo home," the second boy said as he helped his friend to his feet. Together they hobbled off to their bikes.

Rodney stood alone on the valley floor, his face flushed

with anger. Then he had an idea.

Pulling a metal slingshot, complete with wrist brace, from his back pocket, he dug a large stone out of the dirt and slipped the weapon behind his back. His father had bought the slingshot and showed him how to use the powerful elastic to kill birds and squirrels during weekend hunting trips. It was the only bond they shared - a love of killing.

"Hey, Measles," he called out. "Looks like you've won."

Measles popped his head out from behind the old refrigerator.

"It's just me," Rodney called. "You've scared everyone else away."

"You go, too," Measles called back, stepping out from behind his protective metal barrier and walking to the edge of the cliff.

Rodney stared up at Measles and nodded. "You're right," he said. "I know when I'm defeated."

Measles allowed a small smile of victory to cross his face, but it crumbled instantly as Rodney swung his loaded slingshot out from behind his back and fired.

The jagged rock spun through the air so fast that Measles didn't have time to duck. He felt a heavy crack against his forehead as his knees buckled and he crumpled to the ground. A thick river of blood flowed down the left side of his face before he blacked out.

Rodney howled in triumph as he stuck his slingshot back in his pocket and picked up a shovel.

"I'll finish you off later, Measly," Rodney called out to the empty sky. "Once I'm done with your buddy, the freak."

Rodney began to dig.

CHAPTER 11
WHERE'S THE CAVALRY?

"What's he done to Measles?" Owl asked in panic as the sound of digging drew closer.

"I don't know," Joe replied, his face also creased with worry. "But we've got to prepare for when he breaks through."

Quickly, Joe rounded up his troops and began issuing orders, then he noticed the wads of industrial-strength duct tape that were still lying on a rock next to where Owl had been tied up. Instantly, the Japanese Manga warrior was dispatched to retrieve the duct tape while Joe and the others double-checked their arsenal of weapons.

As Joe explained his plan, the other toylings nodded in agreement.

Rodney's shovel broke through the avalanche of mud, expanding the tunnel to the size of a large rabbit.

"I'm going to skin you alive, freak," Rodney threatened as he worked at widening the tunnel some more.

Owl moved as far away from the expanding tunnel as he could, but with the puddle of toxic ooze lapping at the nearby dam he didn't have much room to manoeuvre.

Soon the tunnel was large enough that Rodney threw down the shovel and began to crawl through. When he poked his head into the cavern and saw Owl curled in the corner, a demonic smile twisted his lower lip.

"Knock, knock," he said, pulling his body further into the cavern. "I've huffed and I've puffed and now I'm going to knock your block in."

Owl gulped.

Then a small firecracker fell to the ground in front of

Rodney, its fuse sputtering.

Rodney began to say, "What's tha-" when it exploded in a brilliant flash of light.

Blinded, Rodney tried to rub at his eyes but his hands were too filthy.

"You'll pay for that," he howled in pain.

Rodney felt something land on his head — something with sharp claws and teeth, like a giant metallic insect. Before he could react, a wide band of duct tape was wrapped around his head, covering his eyes.

The Manga warrior flashed a thumbs up to Owl as she leapt from Rodney's head, tucked her body into a somersault and landed on the ground with the grace of an acrobat.

"What's going on!" Rodney screamed as he tried to rip the heavy tape off his face. He stumbled forward, fell over one of the tripwires and toppled face first onto the ground. He missed the puddle of toxic ooze by less than an inch, but his nose inhaled the full effect of its nauseating stench.

Instantly, a dozen tiny feet ran across his back and head, securing his wrists and ankles with more tape.

"Rats! Rats!" Rodney called out in panic. "I'm being eaten by rats."

"Oh be quiet, Rodney," Owl laughed as he helped the toylings secure the tape. "Or I'll get the rats to eat out your tongue." It was a mean thing to say, Owl thought, but Rodney deserved it.

Rodney instantly fell silent, which allowed one of the wrestlers to place a piece of tape across his mouth.

Once they were sure Rodney wasn't going anywhere, Owl and the toylings crawled out the freshly dug tunnel and pulled in lungfuls of the clean night air.

It felt good to be free.

(2)

Owl stretched his muscles and called out Measles' name, but there was no reply.

"I better get up there and find out what's happened to Measles," Owl said.

Joe nodded. "We'll seal up this tunnel. We don't want to panic the polluters before the cavalry gets here."

Owl began to climb up the cliff face as Joe and the other toylings strategically placed the rest of the firecrackers above the tunnel Rodney had dug.

Owl was barely halfway up the cliff when he heard a familiar rumble and turned to see the red and yellow lights of the dump trucks heading into the valley.

"Hurry up, Joe," he called down to the toylings. "They're coming."

Just as he resumed his climb, Owl heard four loud pops followed by the now-familiar sound of falling mud and dirt.

"It's sealed," Joe called out. "We'll meet you at the top."

Picking up the pace, Owl scrambled to get to the top and out of sight before Rodney's dad realized something was amiss.

(3)

At the top of the cliff, Owl ran to Measles' side. His head was badly cut and blood covered half his face.

"Measles," Owl said soothingly. "Can you hear me?"

The redhead groaned and opened one eye. He didn't have the strength to sit up.

"What happen?" he moaned, his voice even thicker than normal.

"Rodney must have hit you with something. Are you

okay?"

"Don't feel good," Measles admitted. "Where's Rodney? How you get out?"

"Don't worry about all that?" Owl said. "Did you contact the authorities? Are they on their way?"

Measles shook his head. "Nobody answered e-mail."

Owl looked crushed. Everything they had gone through was for nothing.

"But," Measles continued. "I bring dad's cell phone. Maybe time call police and firemen."

Owl beamed. "Great job, Measles. Where is it?"

Measles pointed to his zippered pocket. Instantly, Owl dug out the phone, hit the power button and dialed 9-1-1.

When the operator answered, Owl blurted out all his emergencies: a boy had head injuries, another was trapped in a cave, deadly toxic waste was spilling into the ground, the polluters were on site and he needed the police, the fire department and an ambulance right away.

The operator asked for his location and said emergency crews would be dispatched immediately.

"Please hurry," Owl pleaded and hung up.

"Think they come?" Measles asked as the rumbling of the polluters' trucks came closer.

Owl released a heavy sigh. "I sure hope so, friend," he said.

"Friend?" Measles asked. "You mean it?"

Owl laughed. "Do I mean it? Who else would risk their life by standing up to Rodney and his cling-ons, not to mention Rodney's dad and his band of goons, just because I got myself into trouble? Measles, you are the best friend I could ever possibly hope for. We are pals for life, compadre, and don't you ever forget it."

Measles beamed. "You my friend, too, Owl. My friend, too."

(4)

Down below, Rodney's dad unhitched the small backhoe and began digging out the entrance to the cavern.

Dressed in their green and yellow protective gear, the other workers stood around and chatted while they waited for the entrance to be cleared.

Soon, Frank had all the rubble cleared away. He jumped out of the backhoe and walked over to the body of the boy who was lying face down in the dirt. He also noticed the pool of toxic waste and the man-made dam that was keeping it at bay.

Frank laughed. "Well it looks like you were busy," he said. Then he noticed the boy's hands were still taped behind his back.

Frank scratched his head. "How did you manage to build a dam with your hands tied?" he asked.

He rolled the boy over onto his back and got the shock of his life. Instead of the strange-looking snoop he had left in the cavern, the face looking up at him was his own son.

Angrily, he ripped the tape off Rodney's mouth, eyes and wrists.

"What are you doing here?" he yelled.

Rodney groaned in pain as he fought back tears.

"Answer me," his father screamed. "What happened?"

Rodney sniffled. "He had rats helping him."

"Who had rats?"

"Owl. I dug my way in and a bunch of rats attacked me," Rodney sputtered. "He said he was going to get them to eat out my tongue."

"Don't talk nonsense," said his father. "Where's the

freaky kid now?"

"I-I don't know," Rodney said, cowering before his father, just as he had all his life.

Frank instinctively raised his hand to slap Rodney hard across the face when he was stopped by the sound of sirens.

"What have you done?" he gasped, his eyes wide. "You've ruined me!"

"It wasn't me," Rodney howled. "It was Owl."

But Frank wasn't listening; he was too busy racing for his truck to make a quick exit. By the time he reached the cab of his shiny black pickup the fire engines were on site and the police had sealed the only road out.

From high up on the cliff, Owl jumped for joy. Then he turned around to salute Joe and his dirt-encrusted volunteers who were perched on the edge of the old fridge just out of Measles' line of sight.

Joe returned the salute then waved goodbye as he led his team back to their secret village.

"Can we go now?" Measles groaned. "Enough adventure for one day."

Owl grinned down at his friend and nodded. They had both had enough adventure for a while, but today was a day neither of them would soon forget.

CHAPTER 12
IT'S NOT OVER

The next day, every kid in school wanted to shake Owl's hand and slap Measles on the back. News of the polluters and the arrest of Rodney's dad had spread like wildfire through the small community. The mayor had even proclaimed that both Owl and Measles were to be awarded special medals at an upcoming council meeting.

For the first time in his life, Owl knew what it felt like to be popular. But he also knew that most of the people who wanted to shake his hand today were the same people who wouldn't even look at him yesterday.

The exception, of course, being his best friend, Measles, who lapped up the attention like a cat with a fresh bowl of cream. Measles swaggered down the hallway with his head swathed in bandages and his eye beginning to turn a nasty shade of purple. He soaked in the high fives from the boys and the flirtatious glances and winks of the girls.

Measles was in heaven.

In computer class, he fired off a quick message to Owl.

Isn't this great.
What we do next?
- Measles

What do you mean?
- Owl

For encore.
Maybe rock stars.
- Measles

Neither of us is musical.
- Owl

Didn't stop Spice Girls.
- Measles

LOL
True, but I don't think we're quite rock star material.
- Owl

Speak for self.
- Measles

Let's just get through the rest of the month.
We still have to testify in court against Rodney's dad.
That won't be much fun.
- Owl

You kidding?
We star witnesses.
Treat us like gold,
maybe new identities, jobs and cars.
- Measles

We don't have jobs, we can't drive
and I don't think this is exactly a mob trial.
- Owl

We can ask.
- Measles

See you after school, dreamer.
- Owl

Not I see you first.
- Measles

After school, Owl and Measles walked out the front doors surrounded by a mob of people asking a million questions about the capture of the polluters.

Owl and Measles were grinning from ear to ear when the crowd parted to reveal Rodney and his band of cling-ons blocking their way. They were all holding baseball bats.

"It isn't over, Owl," Rodney sneered. "You've put my old man in jail. Did you think I was going to let that slide?"

Owl gulped and Measles placed a hand protectively over his bandaged head.

"There a problem here?" asked a hesitating, but husky voice from behind Owl.

Owl glanced up to see Rocky "Ogre" Malone, the biggest kid in school who towered at least a foot above most of the crowd. Rumor was that Rocky had repeated Grade 6 so many times, he needed to shave twice a day. But because of his size and the way he stood out in a crowd with large ears, an elongated face and a prominent forehead, everyone had been too frightened to ask.

As far as Owl knew, however, Ogre had never done anything to make the other kids so afraid. He tended to keep to himself, reading comic books in the corner of the lunchroom rather than playing soccer or just goofing around on the playground with the rest of them.

Unfortunately, this just made it easier for Rodney and his gang to label him a retard. Owl now knew the use of such a cruel word said more about the person who used it, than the person it was said about.

"This isn't your problem, Ogre," Rodney said, rolling his eyes skyward in an exaggerated gesture to make his cronies laugh. "Go back to your comic books."

"It is my problem," Ogre replied in his slow drawl, placing a large hand on Owl's shoulder. "Owl is my friend."

Owl glanced up at him. "I-I am?" he asked in surprise.

Ogre winked with both eyes and opened his weather-beaten leather jacket to reveal a black T-shirt with a silk-screened image of a humpback whale on it. Above the humpback, in faded, white ink, were the words *Save The Whales*.

"Protect the planet, right?" Ogre said before returning his gaze to Rodney and folding his bulging arms across his chest. "If you have a problem with my friends. . . ," Ogre paused, his face flushing slightly as he strained to collect his words, ". . . you have a problem with me."

Ogre grinned, proud of himself, but to the mouth-gaped crowd it looked like a menacing scowl.

Rodney glanced nervously around at his gang of followers. Ogre had never tried to challenge him before and Rodney didn't have a clue how the giant would react when threatened. All the other kids usually ran away.

"There's a dozen of us and only one of you," Rodney said defiantly, his cruel smile frozen in place.

Ogre grinned, showing all his teeth. "Numbers don't matter," he said, jabbing a meaty finger at Rodney's bony chest. "Your face. My fist." Ogre slammed his fist into his

other hand with a satisfying slap. "That matter."

Rodney winced at the sound of the slap and glanced around at his friends for support, but they suddenly had their heads bowed and eyes diverted as if fascinated with their own shoes. Rodney lowered his bat in defeat. Like most bullies, Rodney had the heart of a chicken.

"This isn't over, Owl," he mumbled, turning his back and beginning to walk away.

"Maybe it is," Ogre called after him.

After Rodney walked away, Owl and Measles released heavy sighs of relief.

"How can we ever thank you, Ogre?" Owl asked, then suddenly paled and blurted quickly, "If it's OK that I call you Ogre."

Ogre smiled shyly. It looked strange on his large, shovel-shaped face. "You call me Ogre. I call you Owl."

Owl sighed in relief. "And this is my friend Measles," he added, gesturing to the redheaded boy who was still trying to stop his knees from shaking.

Measles looked up and stuck out his hand. "Thanks for helping," he said. "I thought we were creamed."

Ogre wrapped his giant hand around Measles' outstretched one and squeezed gently.

"I heard what you did at the dirt," Ogre stopped and wrinkled his brow, angry at choosing the wrong word. "Dump," he said, correcting himself. "I wish I had been there, too."

"Hey, maybe next time," Measles replied as he rubbed his bandaged head, a friendly grin splitting his face. "We need more friends."

Ogre looked shyly at the ground and twirled the dust with his foot.

"I would like that," he said. "I don't have friends." Ogre paused, before adding, "They all are afraid."

"Well you've got friends now," Owl said gleefully as he reached up to pat the large boy's back.

Measles nodded in agreement. "We're going to my home," he said. "Owl says tree fort make awesome clubhouse. Want to join?"

"Join with you?" Ogre asked eagerly.

"Sure," Owl agreed. "You'll be one of the club's founding members."

Ogre grinned. "What do we call ourselves?"

"You said it yourself," answered Owl. "How about The Protectors?"

Ogre gave each of the two boys a stinging high five and together they rode their bikes to what would soon become The Protectors' new clubhouse.

CHAPTER 13
EPILOGUE

Later that night as Owl lay in bed, he heard a sharp tapping at his window.

Quickly, he darted for the window and looked out. At first he couldn't see anything, then he looked down and spotted Joe sitting on the ledge. He lifted the window and the toyling climbed inside.

"I was wondering if I was ever going to see you again," Owl said, sitting down on the edge of his bed. "It all seems like a dream now."

Joe grinned. "Teddy wanted me to deliver the thanks of the village," he said. "All the toylings appreciate what you did for us."

"I'm just glad we stopped it in time," agreed Owl. "The clean-up should be almost complete."

Joe nodded. "We cut it pretty close there. How are you getting on with that Rodney character? He probably didn't appreciate what we did to him."

Owl grinned. "Let's just say I'll need to be a little more careful about hanging out by myself. Luckily, I've made some new friends. We've even started our own club."

"Sounds great," Joe agreed.

"What about you?" Owl asked. "Will I be able to see you again?"

"Hey, we still have to do that John Wayne-Schwarzenegger festival remember?" Joe laughed.

Owl nodded.

Then Joe turned serious. "I'll pop in occasionally when the coast is clear, but it looks like the village might be moving soon."

"Where to?" Owl asked.

"Afraid that's going to have to remain a secret," the toyling said. "The dump is starting to become busier than we like and we have to protect ourselves. If humans get the idea that toylings exist, our village wouldn't stay the haven it needs to be."

"I understand," Owl said. "It's tough being different."

Joe nodded. "I think you're going to do fine, Owl. But if you ever need to get in touch with me just place an action figure on top of your mailbox and I'll find you. Deal?"

"Deal."

Owl and Joe shook finger to hand before the toyling climbed back to the window ledge and disappeared into the night.

Owl curled up in his bed again and closed his eyes.

That night Owl had the most incredible dreams - adventures so alive he could just imagine them all coming true.